Pascal Garnier was born in Paris in 1949. The prize-winning author of more than sixty books, he remains a leading figure in contemporary French literature, in the tradition of Georges Simenon. He died in 2010.

Melanie Florence teaches at the University of Oxford and is a translator from the French.

Praise for Pascal Garnier:

'The combination of sudden violence, surreal touches and bone-dry humour has led to Garnier's work being compared with the films of Tarantino and the Coen brothers, but perhaps more apposite would be the thrillers of Claude Chabrol, a film-maker who could make the ordinary seethe with menace. When the denouement suddenly begins in *The Panda Theory*, it is so unexpected that I read the page twice in shocked disbelief. This might be classed as a genre novel, but Garnier's take on the frailty of life has a bracing originality.' *Sunday Times*

'A small but perfectly formed piece of darkest noir fiction told in spare, mordant prose … Recounted with disconcerting matter-of-factness, this marvellously unpredictable story is surreal and l

'A dark, ric   ng and
brilliant.' *Su*

Boxes

Also by Pascal Garnier:

The Panda Theory
How's the Pain?
The A26
Moon in a Dead Eye
The Front Seat Passenger
The Islanders

Boxes

Pascal Garnier

Translated from the French by Melanie Florence

Gallic Books
London

Garnier,
Pascal

A Gallic Book

First published in France as *Cartons* by Zulma, 2012
Copyright © Zulma, 2012

English translation copyright © Gallic Books 2015
First published in Great Britain in 2015 by Gallic Books, 59 Ebury Street,
London, SW1W 0NZ

A CIP record for this book is available from the British Library
ISBN 978-1-910477-04-5

Typeset in Fournier MT by Gallic Books
Printed in the UK by CPI (CR0 4YY)
2 4 6 8 10 9 7 5 3 1

Brice sat on a metal trunk he had struggled to close, with a silly little rhyme going round and round in his head: 'An old man lived in a cardboard box / With a squirrel, a mouse and a little red fox.' Cardboard boxes: he was completely surrounded by them, in piles stretching from floor to ceiling, so that in order to go from one room to another it was necessary to turn sideways on, like in an Egyptian wall painting. That said, there was no longer any reason to go into another room since, boxes aside, they were all as empty as the fridge and the household drawers. He was the sole survivor of the natural disaster that at one time or another strikes us all, known as moving house.

Following a terrible night's sleep in a room which had already ceased to be his, he had stripped the bed of its sheets, quilt and pillows, and stuffed it all into a big checked plastic bag he had set aside the night before. He had a quick wash, taking care not to spray toothpaste on the mirror, and dutifully inspected the place in case he had forgotten something. But no, apart from a piece of string about a metre and a half long which he unthinkingly wound round his hand, there was nothing left but the holes made by nails and screws which had held up picture frames or shelves. For a brief moment he thought of hanging himself with the piece of string but gave up the idea. The situation was painful enough already.

There was still a good hour before Breton Removals would come to put an end to ten years of a life so perfect that it seemed it would last for ever.

That cold November morning he was furious with Emma for having left him helpless and alone, in the hands of the removal men, who in an hour's time would descend like a swarm of locusts to ransack the apartment. Both strategically and psychologically, his position was untenable, so he decided to go out for a coffee while he waited for the world to end.

The neighbourhood seemed already to have forgotten him. He saw no one he knew, with the result that, instead of going to his usual bistro, he chose one he had never set foot in before. Above the bar, a host of notices informed the clientele that the telephone was reserved for customers, the use of mobiles was strongly discouraged, it would be wise to beware of the dog and, of course, no credit would be given. A guy with dyed red-blond hair came in, issuing a general 'Hi!' He was some sort of actor or comedian Brice had seen on TV. For a good few minutes he tried unsuccessfully to remember his name, then since this quest – as annoying as it was futile – led nowhere, he persuaded himself he had never known it. Behind him, wafts of disinfectant and urine came from the toilet doorway, mingling with the smell of coffee and dead ashtrays. A sort of black tide made his stomach heave at the first mouthful of espresso. He sent a few coins spinning on to the bar and made his escape, a bent figure with turned-up collar.

In the stairway he passed Monsieur Pérez, his upstairs neighbour.

'Today's the day, then?'

'Yes, I'm just waiting for the removal men.'

'It'll seem strange for you, living in the countryside.'

'A little, no doubt, to begin with.'

'And particularly in your situation. Speaking of which, still no news of your lady?'

'I'm hopeful.'

'That's good. I'm very partial to the countryside, but only for holidays, otherwise I don't half get bored. Well, each to his own. Right then, good luck, and keep your chin up for the move. It's just something you have to get through.'

'Have a good day, Monsieur Pérez.'

For the past month Brice had felt like someone with a serious illness. Everyone talked to him as if he were about to have an operation, with the feigned empathy of hospital visitors. That moron Pérez was going off to work just as he had done every morning for years, and in the evening, after doing his shopping at the usual places, he would collapse, blissfully happy, on to his trusty old sofa in front of the TV, snuggling into his usual routine, sure of his immortality. At that moment, Brice would have loved to be that moron Pérez.

Breton Removals were barely five minutes late when they rolled up, but it seemed an eternity to him as he waited, leaning at the window and smoking one cigarette after another. It was a huge white lorry, a sort of refrigerated vehicle. Naturally, in spite of the official notices reserving the space between such and such times, a BMW had flouted the rules and parked right outside his apartment. The four Bretons (only one of whom actually was, Brice learned later) shifted the car in five minutes flat, as easily as if it had been a bicycle. Supremely indifferent to the chorus of car horns behind them, they took their time manoeuvring into position, displaying with their Herculean strength the utmost disdain for the rest of humanity.

This was a crack fighting unit, a perfectly oiled machine, a band of mercenaries to whom Brice had just entrusted his life. He was simultaneously reassured and terror-struck. He took the precaution of opening the door in case they took it off its hinges when they knocked.

As in all good criminal bands, the shortest one was

the leader. Mind you, what Raymond lacked in height he made up for in width. He looked like an overheated Godin stove. Perhaps it was an occupational hazard, but they were each reminiscent of a piece of furniture: the one called Jean-Jean, a Louis-Philippe chest of drawers; Ludo, a Normandy wardrobe; and the tall, shifty-looking one affectionately known as The Eel, a grandfather clock. This outfit of rascals with bulging muscles and smiles baring wolf-like teeth made short work of surveying the flat. Each of them exuded a smell of musk, of wild animal escaped from its cage. Strangely, Brice felt safe, as if he had bought himself a personal bodyguard. From that moment, however, came the nagging question: how much of a tip should he give?

In no time at all, the heavies toured the apartment, made an expert estimate of the volume of furniture and boxes, and concluded, 'No problem. Let's get on with it.' And they set to with a will. Chests of drawers, wardrobes, tables and chairs were transformed by grey sheets into unidentifiable objects, disappearing one by one as if by magic, whereas, a few years earlier, Brice had sweated blood getting them in. Ditto with the boxes, which for the past month he had struggled to stack, and which now seemed to have no weight at all on the removal men's shoulders. Despite the graceful little sideways jumps Brice executed to avoid them, each worker in his own way made it clear that he had no business getting under their feet: they knew what they were doing. At that point, the existential lack of purpose which had dogged him from earliest childhood assumed monumental proportions, and he suggested going to fetch them cold drinks.

'Beer?'

'Oh no! Orangina, or mineral water, still.'

Even rogues went on diets, did they?

The Arab man who ran the corner shop where Brice bought his alcohol was most surprised to see him buying such tame drinks.

'What's this, boss? Are you ill?'

'No, it's for the removal men.'

'That's it then; you're leaving us?'

'That's life.'

'What about your wife? Still no news?'

'I'm hopeful.'

'We'll miss you, boss.'

Clearly, given the amount of money Brice handed over to him in a month, the man had every reason to regret his departure.

On his return to the apartment, nothing remained but the bed and the flock of grey fluff balls grazing along the skirting boards.

'That was quick!'

'We're pros. We don't hang around.'

The Eel's back was drenched in sweat. With the well-worn blade of his pocket knife, he cut the excess from a length of twine tied round what must have been a TV. Hemp fibres floated for a moment in the emptiness of the apartment. Raymond appeared, grabbing a can of Orangina which he downed in one. He let out a long, loud burp and wiped his lips with the back of his hand.

'Bloody intellectuals! You shouldn't pile up boxes of books like that.'

'I'm sorry, I didn't know.'

'Well, you do now.'

After this glittering riposte, Raymond the Stove handed him a green sheet, a pink sheet and a yellow sheet, jabbing his index finger at the exact spot where Brice had to sign.

'Right, Lyon to Valence, best allow a good hour. Since we'll be having a snack en route, let's say two-thirty in your little village.'

'I'll be waiting for you.'

'Fine. See you in a bit.'

Brice felt something tighten in his chest at the slightly too manly handshake and, as he closed the front door behind him for the last time, he had a vague idea of what a heart attack would be like. There, it was over. Brice was quite stunned. He recalled the anecdote about a man who was about to have his head chopped off by an executioner famed for his skill.

'Please, Monsieur le bourreau, make a good job of it.'

'But I've done it, Monsieur!'

The stakes for the vines, black like burnt matchsticks and set in serried rows on the hillside, were reminiscent of some sort of military cemetery. Despite its name, Saint-Joseph's Grande Rue was so narrow you could have clasped hands with your neighbour on the other side. The enterprise would have been futile, mind you, given all the blank façades with their closed shutters and bolted doors. No activity, not so much as a cat or dog, nothing except a bakery, which was shut that day, and a pharmacy at the entrance to the village. Its green cross, framed in the rear-view mirror, promised little in the way of entertainment. Only a sign stuck at a street corner pointing to 'Martine Coiffure: Ladies' and Gents' Hair Salon' might, at a pinch, suggest a modicum of frivolity. Otherwise, there was nothing but vineyard signs emblazoned with badly painted bunches of grapes, creaking to and fro on both sides of the road.

From within the stone church tower, which stood out against the grey-green wash of sky, the bell struck one with a deafening clang as Brice was drawing up outside the house, *his* house. Round one could begin.

'What the hell am I doing here? What on earth possessed us to buy this dump? I must have been drunk. That's it, I was drunk.'

The house seemed enormous, far bigger than when he had visited it two months earlier with Emma.

'So, dining room and kitchen there, sitting room here, opening on to the terrace. On the first floor the bedrooms, bathroom (with a bath and two washbasins), study, and then, in the attic, your studio. Aren't the beams magnificent? You'll be able to work so well here!'

All Brice could recall of that visit were fragments, like those which come back to you from a long-gone dream. It was dark, and he was hungry and tired. The estate agent, squeezed into his cheap little pinstriped suit, had followed them round like a poodle and, since he had no sales pitch, turned on all the electric light switches – *clickety click* – to prove that everything had been redone.

'Well, darling?'

To make the question go away, and with no thought for the consequences, he had said yes. In the car, Emma had taken him through in endless and minute detail the innumerable plans she had in mind for decorating, to turn the cavern into a veritable palace.

'And did you see it's all been completely redone? The electricity …'

'That's right. *Clickety click.*'

Now stone walls and ceilings weighed down by enormous beams were leaning in on him, menacingly. It was extremely cold, and dim like in a cave. He opened the blinds in the dining room and living room, but the dishwater-coloured light which poured in did nothing to warm the atmosphere. It was like being in an aquarium without the fish.

'A burial plot for life, that's what we've bought ourselves.'

He went from room to room, forming a cross with his body at each window as his outspread arms flung the shutters wide. From outside he might have been taken for a Swiss cuckoo clock. *Bong*, the church clock struck the half-hour on his head.

He set the electricity meter going, turned on the water heater and put on all the lights. Then, as there was no chair, he sat down on the stairs. There was something suspicious: the house had no smell, not even of damp, as is usual in houses which have been empty for months on end. Apart from some arachnid presences among the beams – and not many, at that – there was no sign of life. For the first time in his existence he was an owner. But an owner of what? Of an empty universe, round which the crackling of the match struck for his cigarette echoed in a semblance of the Big Bang.

The removal men were on time. At exactly half past

two – the church clock testified to that – the giant lorry occupied the Grande Rue. The four Atlases were in a cheerful mood.

'Your little village is nice. It makes a change for us from estates and high-rises in Vénissieux or Villeurbanne. There it is, then. Wow, your house is big!'

'Yes, it is rather on the large side.'

'And you'll be living here all on your own?'

'No, my wife's joining me.'

'Even for two, it's really big. Right … Let's get on with it, lads, shall we?'

Brice felt quite emotional at seeing them again. It was as if a boat had made landfall on his desert island. The man who had always been too proud to join a band, a group, any association whatsoever, found himself savouring the unquantifiable joy of merging into this mass of humans, one atom among many.

After taking the men on a quick tour of the house, Brice stationed himself at the entrance to the garage and, as each of the large items appeared before him, pronounced with the confidence of a man who knows what he's about: 'Dining room', 'Living room', 'Yellow bedroom', 'Blue bedroom', 'Study', 'Studio' and so on. As for the countless boxes marked 'Kitchen', 'Bathroom', 'Clothes', 'Books' and particularly those which, as their contents were unknown, were labelled vaguely 'Misc.', he had them piled up in the garage. They could be dealt with later. It took only a couple of hours. Once the essentials – beds, wardrobes, chests of drawers, tables, armchairs and sofas – had found appropriate places, it began to look like a real house. That is to say, you could sit in different parts of it, eat and maybe even sleep there.

'There you are, home.'

'Is that it?'

'Well, yes.'

Brice was struggling to get used to the idea that they were going, leaving him on his own. He was gripped by a sort of panic.

'There's a café on the main road. Can I buy you a drink?'

'That's kind, but we need to get back. We've a life outside the job.'

'Of course, I quite understand.'

Raymond proudly refused the tip Brice proffered, but consented to shake his hand. With the fifty-euro note still in his hand, and a tear in his eye, he watched the lorry manoeuvre then disappear round the corner of the road. A few drops of rain splashed down at his feet, and spread like ink on blotting paper. No two fell in the same spot.

That evening he had to eat, not out of greed or pleasure, but simply because unless a human being takes nourishment, he dies. In the garage he counted no fewer than eleven boxes which belonged in the kitchen and – surprise, surprise – most of them were behind the ones filled with books, which he had to move at the risk of hurting his back. Emma was unreasonably fond of kitchenware. There was enough to fit out a restaurant: plates of all sizes, soup tureens, sauce boats, fruit bowls, tea and coffee services; dishes for tarts, fish and asparagus; dishes made of silver, porcelain and earthenware; water glasses, wine glasses, whisky glasses; canteens of cutlery both antique and contemporary; sets of saucepans, cast-iron casserole dishes, a wok, a rice cooker, a tagine … and all in pristine condition for the good reason that Emma never cooked, and preferred to invite friends to a restaurant rather than entertain them at home. The yoghurt maker, blender and various other gadgets had not even made it out of their original packaging. When it was just the two of them, something frozen went into the microwave and … *ping!*

Box after box was slashed open with a Stanley knife in his search for a tin of food. Every five minutes, the light switch would time out and he would have to feel his way back across the garage to put it on again, bumping his foot or his shin against the scattered boxes. At last he found a tin, pike quenelles in 'Nantua sauce', only a few weeks past their use-by date. Sadly the tin was lacking the handy little ring which would have allowed him to free the contents without the aid of a tin-opener. The search through the boxes resumed, increasingly frantic now. Aside from a bottle of Bordeaux, he found virtually everything he did not need: pastry wheel, ice-cream scoop, nutcrackers, cake slice, olive pitter, snail tongs – but the tin-opener still evaded detection. Yet they did have one, he was sure of it, a fancy streamlined model which was the work of a famous designer, and not in fact terribly practical. They had bought it at vast expense in a specialist shop across from Les Halles in Lyon.

Brice had first met Emma at a gallery during the private view of a Hungarian artist whose 'thing' was using varnish to fossilise the remains of goulash on plates. His work wasn't bad, it just all looked the same. It was like an oven in the gallery packed with goulash lovers. The women's perfumes mingled with the men's sweat to produce a noxious mixture. Brice went outside and leant against the wing of a yellow Fiat, sipping lukewarm rosé from a plastic cup. One by one, people left the gallery, dripping with sweat like survivors of some kind of shipwreck, the men loosening their ties and the women slipping a finger into their low necklines. A tall, rangy brunette whose hair was pinned up with a pencil came to sit next to him, fanning herself with her invitation.

'It's like a sauna in there!'

'Unbearable.'

'Did you like it?'

'What?'

'The show.'

'Oh … In this heat I'm not overly keen on goulash.'

She laughed. A nose just sufficiently bent to miss perfection, dark eyes spangled with green, a perfectly ripe mouth, hardly any bust and unusually long, narrow feet which reminded him of pointed slippers.

'Well, it's given me an appetite. I could eat a raw elephant.'

'Luckily I know a restaurant where that's the speciality.'

She hesitated for a moment, dangling one of her mules from her toes, before turning to him with a serious expression. 'Are you sure their elephants are fresh?'

'I can guarantee it; they're picked every morning.'

'Good. Is it a long way?'

'No, in Africa. There's a bush-taxi rank on the corner.'

'I'd prefer to take my car.'

'Where is it?'

'We're sitting on it.'

The yellow Fiat took them to a pleasant restaurant in La Croix-Rousse, where, in the absence of elephants, they tucked into grilled king prawns under an arbour festooned with multicoloured lanterns. Once they had got the small talk out of the way, they spent a wonderful night in Emma's bed. Three months later Brice Casadamont, illustrator, made Emma Loewen, journalist, his lawfully wedded wife at the town hall in Lyon's sixth arrondissement. It was as simple as ABC. It was time. Puffed out from fast living, Brice was limping painfully towards his fifties, while Emma was frolicking through her thirties, as lithe as a gazelle. He spent months trying to understand how this young gilded adventurer could have fallen for an old creature like him. She was beautiful, healthy, passionate about her work, made more money than him – what did he have to offer her but memories of a time when perhaps he had been someone, and promises of a glorious future in which he had obviously long since stopped believing? But women's hearts are as unfathomable and full of oddities as the bottom of their handbags. Occasionally he would ask her, 'Why me, Emma?' She would smile and, with a kiss, call him an old fool, pack her case and go off to report from Togo, or Tanzania, or somewhere else. At first, with every trip he was afraid he would never see her again but, strangely, she always came back. He had to get used to the idea that she loved him. This was their life, no matter that it raised a few eyebrows. She came and went. He stayed put, persisting in painting unsaleable canvases more out of habit than enjoyment, and earning derisory sums from illustrating deadly dull children's books.

Once more the timer plunged him into darkness, but now that he was used to it, he nimbly dodged the obstacles. Giving up on the tin-opener, he got hold of a sharp knife and went back up to the kitchen.

It seemed to him that a hint of warmth was beginning to spread through the space. The radiators were tepid. That said, it would have been unwise to discard his reefer jacket and woolly hat just yet. After a battle with the tin of quenelles, a process in which he almost gashed his hand at least ten times, he ate dinner at the corner of the table, half listening to the news on France Inter. Bombs were going off almost everywhere in the world.

On the pretext of fighting the cold, but chiefly to take the edge off the emptiness surrounding him, he had finished the bottle of wine, and it was when his forehead touched the table that he took the wise decision to go to bed still fully dressed, rolled up in a dust cover the removal men had left behind. The church clock hammered eleven times, using his head as an anvil.

'That's not too hot, is it?'

'No, it's fine.'

Martine's strong fingers were not only massaging his scalp, they were giving his brain a good kneading, and Brice was thoroughly enjoying it. The thousand and one domestic worries which had in recent days sprung forth from his skull like water through the holes in a colander were now merging into a soft paste not dissimilar to the origin of the world, when every embryo was unaware even of its own existence.

'Right, if you'd like to follow me ...'

He let himself be shown to the swivel chair and draped in a huge black nylon robe which completely obscured the lines of his body.

'Short?'

'Er … Yes, well, not too short.'

'It's strange. I feel I know you.'

'But it's the first time I've been here.'

'Yes, you said. It must be from seeing all those faces go past. In the end they merge into one.'

He surrendered himself to Martine's hands while his upturned eyes sneaked a good look at her in the mirror facing him. She had reached the age when a woman's sugar turns to honey. An inviting bosom in a tight black T-shirt with a spangled Pierrot embroidered on it formed the base to a neckless doll-like face plastered with make-up which gave her plump cheeks the shiny satin look of artificial fruit. The features were brought to life by two obsidian pupils shaded by extravagant false lashes, with a piercing gaze that went straight to your wallet. Two-tone hair, platinum blonde and Day-Glo pink, crowned a forehead crossed by a worry line which no face cream could shift. A garlic-tinged accent emerged from lips picked out with a thick garnet line.

'Well now, so you're the one who's taken the Loriol house?'

'Yes.'

'It's a beautiful house, and renovated top to bottom. I must say, a builder like Loriol knows how to go about it. *And* he's a shrewd one, knows all the tricks. If you'd seen how it was before, a real wreck. I have to say, old Janin, the previous owner, was no good for anything after his wife died, let everything go to rack and ruin.

He spent more time in the cellar than he did in the rest of the house, if you take my meaning. Poor old thing … Loriol must have got it for a song.'

The cellar. He had been down there for the first time the day before. A lovely vaulted cellar with walls covered in saltpetre and a trodden earth floor. He had stayed there for some time, sitting on a crate, looking at the double ceiling hook which in olden days had been used for hanging the pig. By concentrating hard enough he had ended up seeing the pig, head downwards, split open, offering up the unfathomable mystery of its entrails as in a Soutine painting. Seized by an irresistible force, he had grasped the iron hooks and, with knees bent, had swung there until his hands lost their grip. For three days he had been putting off the countless administrative procedures entailed by a house move: electricity, telephone, change of address, gas, water, bank … Normally it was Emma who took care of these chores. She would have had it all sorted in two shakes of a lamb's tail, whereas he broke into a sweat, eyes watering, ears buzzing, if faced with the simplest form to fill in. No way out but to go and hang from a hook in a cellar ceiling. Old Janin must have felt this same deep distress after his wife died.

'Did he hang himself?'

'No, his liver gave out on him.'

'Oh. What was his wife's name?'

'Marthe, I think.'

'And were they very much in love?'

'No, they used to row the whole time, but that's normal. There you are, all nice and handsome.'

In the mirror Martine was holding up behind him, he noticed the skin on his neck reddened by shaving burn. The neck of a hanged man.

'That's perfect, thank you.'

A cloud of white hairs floated up round him as Martine relieved him of the robe.

'You've a good type of hair, thick but slightly dry. I've a very effective lotion, if you'd like.'

'Um, OK. Why not?'

Every time he got out of the hands of a hairdresser he was in such a vulnerable state that he could be sold anything at all, at no matter what price – something those seasoned professionals were not slow to sniff out and exploit.

While Brice was waiting for his change, a curious apparition made the little bell on the door ring.

'Hello, Blanche. I'll be right with you.'

Blanche lived up to her name, being dressed in white from the toes of her shoes right up to her strange crocheted lace cap which reminded him of a tea cosy. All in white, but an off-white bordering on old ivory. She was like a bride who had been in the shop window for too long. It was difficult to put an exact age on her; she could have been anywhere between sixteen and sixty, depending on whether you looked at her eyes, which were like those of a timid child, or her hands, gloved in skin like puckered silk.

Instead of making a beeline for the dog-eared magazines littering the coffee table, as any other female client would, she stayed standing, twisting a little purse embroidered with pearl beads in her impossibly delicate fingers. Her eyes were fixed on Brice. It made him vaguely uneasy.

'So, Monsieur. Welcome to Saint-Joseph!'

Outside, the north wind grabbed the back of his neck with its icy fingers. Through the curtain veiling the window, he saw Martine take Blanche by the arm and lead her gently to the washbasin, where she sat down, leaning back so abruptly that it looked as if an invisible hand had just snapped her in two. On his way from the hair salon to the post office he could not rid himself of that immaculate vision imprinted like a negative on his retina.

In the post office, three elderly ladies were waiting at the counter – one big, one middle-sized and one small, all so alike it was tempting to think of slipping them one inside the other like Russian dolls. The saving in space would have been advantageous as the place was minuscule. Four customers was definitely one too many. Brice squeezed himself up against the wall as best he could, between a missing persons notice depicting a curly-headed cherub and an advertisement for a loan with unbeatable rates. One after the other, each babushka exchanged with the postmistress news of their respective states of health. The talk was of hernia bandages, support stockings, varicose veins, rheumatism, prolapses, and other of life's small mishaps, punctuated by the sound of documents being stamped, and this for a good half-hour. At last it was his turn. Not yet on sufficiently intimate terms with the postmistress to mention the ravages wrought by time on his own body, he confined himself to asking for a packet of cards, intended to inform people of his change of address. Éliette (that was the postmistress's sweet name) had the ashen complexion of a consumptive heroine. No doubt her screen was not up to the job of protecting her from her customers' germ-ridden breath. She broke into a wan smile as she handed him a bundle of cards and, raising an eyelid like a withered iris petal, turned a watery gaze towards him.

'Are you the gentleman who's taken over the Loriol house?'

'Yes, that's me.'

'Do you have relatives here?'

'But … No … Why?'

'You look like a gentleman who used to live here. The family goes back generations. Welcome to Saint-Joseph, then.'

He thought he detected a touch of irony in the little phrase which she breathed out like a last sigh.

The days went by, or was it perhaps the same one again and again? Other than a minimum of maintenance – eating, drinking, sleeping – which necessitated brief commando raids on the supermarket, Brice did nothing. Not once had he gone up to the studio, nor into the other rooms, for that matter. He had adopted the stance of the monitor lizard: total immobility, eyelids half closed, prepared to wait for centuries for its prey – that is, a sign from Emma – to come along. He was becoming inured to boredom as others are to opium. Elbows on the table littered with dirty plates and cutlery, the remains of charcuterie in greasy paper, and wine glasses with a coating of red, he would leaf through his address book, yawning. Except for a few professional connections useful to his survival, he saw no one he should inform of his new contact details. Acquaintances, he had those, of course, but friends? They all seemed to belong to a bygone world, for which he no longer felt the slightest nostalgia. Under each of the names he scored through in red, a face would dissolve, its blurred outlines overflowing the page and calling to mind only faint, drowned continents. He experienced neither remorse nor regret. They had had their time. He had new friends now, called Martine, Blanche, Éliette, Babushka. Only women. Obviously, since in the daytime the village was transformed into a no man's land. From dawn to dusk the able-bodied men were engaged in obscure and mysterious occupations. Occasionally you might come across an old man on a rickety bicycle in a back street, carrying a crate of cabbages or leeks. Otherwise it was women, nothing but women. Practical, solid women, women you could rely on, with short hair and loose-fitting clothes. In the mornings they would walk the children to school, picking up bread and the newspaper, exchanging two or three pieces of gossip before hurrying off to their respective homes to get on with the countless chores in house or garden which would keep them busy until evening. What might the inner lives of these housewives be like? By what dreams were they haunted? What secrets were they hiding?

Brice was at that point in his reflections when a loose slip of paper drifted out of his address book. He recognised Emma's rounded handwriting. She had made a note of the various places she wanted to put up shelves. It was ridiculous how fond women were of shelves. All those he had known had made him put them up when they moved in. It had to be some sort of initiation rite. To be honest, he had never really been excited by that sort of activity, but anything to drag himself out of the dull apathy into which his lunch of tripe à la Provençale had plunged him. It was time to take some measurements, he told himself, braving the garage in search of a tape measure.

Currently the garage looked like nothing on earth. It was as if some sort of typhoon had laid waste the pyramids of boxes built with such care by the removal men. Odd items of clothing flopped like stranded seaweed over piles of crockery, books fanning open, and scattered CDs, which he had to pick his way over like a heron. The wreck resulted from the simple fact that, in order to lay your hands on some vital object (which very often was still not found), it was necessary to fight your way through a mountain of this, that and the other with an energy born of desperation. If the first few boxes had been meticulously packed and labelled, most of the others, marked 'Misc.', simply contained a jumble of things he had no idea even existed. And the more of them he uncovered, the more the confusion grew, until it was no longer possible to tell one thing from another. Only chance could be of any help. And it was thanks to chance that he came upon his DIY kit, after he had toppled a shoebox which hit the floor, pouring out a stream of seashells. He crushed some in regaining his balance, and set about making an inventory of his tools:

one hammer minus its shaft, one twisted screwdriver, two baby-food jars (spinach and ham, apple and pear) half full of nails, screws, drawing pins, rubber bands and wall plugs, a Stanley knife without a blade, a gummed-up paint brush, rusty pincers, a ball of string, a roll of sticky tape, two jam-jar lids and, yes, a flexible steel rule, one of those that joiners carry proudly in the special little pocket on the right leg of their overalls. In view of the overwhelming task Emma had entrusted to him, these materials were clearly insufficient. For an hour he sat in the dark, bursting countless blisters of bubble wrap, unable to convince himself of the necessity of a sortie to the nearest Bricorama. DIY superstores were beyond the pale to him, as much a no-go area as a locker room. In any case, if he did have to steel himself to it, it was too late for today. That kind of expedition was undertaken in the early morning, like hunting or fishing. Anyway, he didn't feel prepared – he had to make a list, take measurements. That was it, first the measurements!

Armed with the steel rule, he began measuring anything and everything, the width of doors, the length of handles, his left forearm, the wingspan of a beetle squashed at the bottom of the sink that morning, the height of the sink, the depth of a box of camembert, and its diameter. And so on until late into the night, when he finally stopped, worn out, but dazzled at knowing the dimensions of his universe down to the last millimetre. It was then that he remembered all the catalogues and brochures which cluttered up his letter box every morning. Screw-It-All, DIY Super-Something – the bin was stuffed full of them. He ran to get them and began poring over them compulsively until dawn, when sleep carried him off to a universe inhabited by 2,000-watt blowtorches, tilting jigsaws, orbital sanders with dust bags and large-sized sanding sheets.

The timbre of the church bell varied, depending on the wind. It ranged from the whine of an electric saw to the radiating waves of a gong. Thus it not only told the time, but what kind of day it was. Today was a gong day, with a heavy bronze sky that weighed down on you. Brice had indeed gone to Brico-whatsit as planned, but once he had parked in the car park and seen the never-ending coming and going of the half-man, half-bear creatures shifting heavy loads – wooden beams, metal rails, bags of cement, oil cans – he was gripped by a kind of terror which paralysed him for a good fifteen minutes. It brought back memories of military service, or the area around a stadium, or anywhere men were all together. He refused to turn back, however, and, in awkward imitation of the lumbering gait of a man who knows what he has to do, he ventured head down into the store.

They had thought of everything here. There were all sorts of screws, hammers to drive nails into corners, saws for cutting on the diagonal, glues for sticking anything to everything, spiral staircases that could be put up in ten seconds, paints to hide every sin, real wood, fake wood, marvellous tools for weird and wonderful purposes, and all of them beautiful, red, yellow, green and chrome, like Christmas toys. Brice had no idea what to choose. He went for a five-kilo sledgehammer on sale for next to nothing. It was the first time he had bought a five-kilo sledgehammer. He was more than a little proud. Emma would certainly have approved of his purchase.

Nothing is as soothing as watching a saucepan of water come to the boil. Brice had just plunged two eggs into the merrily moving bubbles when the phone rang for the first time since he had lived there. The sound was so incongruous that he reacted only at the fourth ring. The girl on the line was nervously offering him a wonderful fitted kitchen. Brice declined, and thanked her. No sooner had he hung up than the phone was gripped anew by the same noisy fever, making the house tremble from cellar to attic.

'Hello, is that Brice?'

'Yes.'

'It's Myriam. How are you?'

That was quite a question his mother-in-law had landed on him.

'Oh, fine, fine.'

'You're sure?'

'Well, you know, when you've just moved into a new house it's always a little …'

'Oh, I quite understand. You know, Simon and I are thinking of you.'

'That's kind.'

'It's all so … so … We were thinking of dropping by this weekend.'

'Oh, I'd love that, but the house isn't ready yet. There's still a lot to do and …'

'Exactly. We could give you a hand. You know how keen on DIY Simon is. And I'm sure you could use a woman for your washing and cooking. We all know what a man on his own is like.'

'Honestly, I'm managing very well. I'm just putting up some shelves. Emma would be cross to think I'd entertained you in a building site. I've no wish to get told off when she comes back.'

'Brice.'

'Yes?'

'Are you still taking the medication Dr Boaert prescribed?'

'Of course.'

'Brice … you need help. You know quite well we're

going through the same as you. You mustn't let yourself go. We'll be stronger, the three of us together. I'm sure Emma would have agreed with me. Brice?'

Silence.

'Brice, are you listening to me?'

'Yes, Myriam. I'm sorry but I have some eggs on the stove. I'll have to hang up now.'

'Think about what I'm saying, Brice. We're very fond of you.'

'Me too, Myriam. Give Simon a hug from me. Thanks. I'll call you soon!'

He threw down the receiver as if it were a dead animal and unplugged the cord.

Emma's picture joined the other photos scattered at his feet like a game of solitaire sprinkled with egg shells. He felt a heaviness in his stomach and stretched out on the camp bed he had set up just beside the boiler. If the truth be known, apart from the kitchen, toilet and bathroom, he scarcely went into the other rooms any more. What was the use of making hundreds of trips to and fro in order to distribute all these things, when he knew that Emma would rearrange them all when she got back? It was easier to settle down in their midst. The icy glow of the fluorescent light, whose timer switch he had craftily deactivated with a piece of sticky tape, didn't bother him in the least, day or night. A kind of trench dug through the bric-a-brac allowed him to reach the staircase. It was enough. Thanks to this makeshift arrangement, he had everything within reach. This set-up was so much more practical, and it was obvious the objects had accepted him as one of their own.

That morning in the post, among a pile of brochures advertising monster sales with prices cut, slashed, pared to the bone, there had been a letter from his editor who, while sympathising deeply with his situation, informed him of the urgent need to submit the final drawings for *Sabine Does Something Silly*. He would be eternally grateful if Brice could deliver them within a week.

Brice could no longer bear the little girl, still less her creator, Mabel Hirsch. Admittedly the two of them had been his bread and butter for a number of years now, but after about ten volumes he had had enough: *Sabine Loses Her Dog, Sabine Takes on Dracula, Sabine Sets Sail, Sabine* … The little brat, whose face he riddled with freckles for sport, was seriously taking over his life. As for her creator, he must have killed her at least a hundred times in the course of troubled dreams. He would throttle her until her big frogspawn eyes burst out of their sockets and then tear off all her jewellery. She could no longer move her poor arthritic fingers, they were so weighed down with gold and diamonds. Strings of pearls disappeared into the soft fleshy folds of her double chin. Old, ugly and nasty with it! All that emerged from her scar of a mouth, slathered in blood-red honey, were barbed compliments which wound themselves round your neck, the better to jab you in the back. The widow of a senior civil servant, she had never had to earn a living. Yet she was one of the publishing house's top sellers. Dominique Porte, the director, put up with the worst humiliations from her, and consequently so did Brice. How many times had she made him do the same illustration over and over again, only to come back to the first one in the end? And yet, according to what she told anyone who would listen, she adored him. That was perhaps true in a sense, for they both had a hatred of childhood, only for different reasons. She had probably never experienced it, while Brice had still not succeeded in leaving it behind.

In the early days of his marriage to Emma, friends had warned him, 'She's thirty, she'll be wanting to make a father out of you!' They were wrong. He and Emma had barely so much as touched on the subject. Emma had nothing against children – other people's, that is. When they visited friends who had children, she showed affectionate interest, never appearing to tire of playing silly games with them, but when it was time to go, no sooner had the car moved off than she gave a sigh of relief.

Her friends and family were astonished by this state of affairs. To them it seemed abnormal that any perfectly healthy young woman should not wish to play mummy. Perhaps it was because of her career, having to jet off on trips at a moment's notice, or perhaps one of the two was sterile. Brice and Emma laughed it off, content to leave their secret veiled by an artistic blur. The truth was so much simpler than that. Their love bound them together so closely that the smallest seed, the tiniest embryo would have come between them.

Children had always frightened him, even when he was one himself. Those signs on the way into villages: 'Beware Children!' How were they to be interpreted? He feared them like the plague.

'Children are ogres, vampires. You only have to look at their young parents – the mothers with their dried-up breasts, the empty-handed fathers – to grasp the sheer greed of these merciless cannibals. They get us in the prime of life and ruin our secret gardens with their red tricycles and bouncy balls that flatten everything like wrecking balls. They transform our lovers into fat women, drooling blissfully as they feel their bellies, and turn us into idiots numb with exhaustion, pushing supermarket trolleys overflowing with bland foodstuffs. They get angry with us because they're midgets, obliging us to punish them and then regret it. On the beach they play at burying us or dig holes to push us into. That's all they dream of: taking our place. They're ashamed of us, are sorry they're not orphans, but still ape us horribly. Later they ransack our drawers, and become more and more stupid as their beards grow, their breasts grow, their teeth grow. Soon, like past years, we no longer see them. They'll reappear only to chuck a handful of earth or a withered rose on to our coffin and argue over the leftovers. Children are Nazis; they recognise only one race: their own.'

The editor's letter came to rest on a pile of envelopes he had not bothered to open. He stretched out on his camp bed and said to himself that this would be a good day to die.

He was drowsing, drowsing, and then, quite without warning, he opened his eyes and woke up as someone different, someone who was having nothing more to do with Sabine, in this life or the next. It had just struck four, and it was still light. The hard-boiled eggs still lay heavy in his stomach and so it occurred to him to aid his digestion by going for a short walk in the open air for the first time since he had arrived. The choice on leaving his place was simple: either you went left and after 500 metres you hit the main road, where the terrifying articulated lorries would be more than happy to flatten a pedestrian, or you went right, taking the path that wound past the church, up among the vines. Naturally, that was the one he took, whistling to himself. Not for long. The section leading out of the village presented no problems, but very soon the slope became so steep it felt like scaling a vertical wall. His smart tan suede loafers were far from suited to this kind of terrain, muddy, full of pebbles and deep cracks. Every other step he stumbled, tripped and slid, enjoying none of the benefits of nature. He had to sit down to remove a stone from his left shoe. Vine stalks, twisted like the hoofs of a sick billy goat, clung to grey wooden posts; banks of brambles coiled beside the path like barbed wire; straggly trees pleaded with the sky, an occasional mocking crow perched on a branch; and the worst of it was this bitch of a red, slippery soil. There was nothing to stop him turning back except men's obstinate need to see things through to the very end. He set off again, sliding on this Way of the Cross with no station at which to get off.

A quarter of an hour later, exhausted and covered in mud, just as he was extracting a crown of thorns' worth of spines from his palm, he heard the sound of a spring on his left. It was coming from a sort of gap in the undergrowth. Drawn on, as in a fairy tale, he ventured in. Despite the pitfalls, treacherous roots, half-buried stones, holes and mounds, nothing on earth could now have prevented him from getting closer to this primal gurgling; it had become as essential to him as a teat to a newborn baby. It was as he came round the final turn that he caught sight of it, new, exposed, gushing forth from the granite lips. The water, thick like a cordial, greasy like oil, flung the sky's image back at it in a magnificent act of defiance.

From pool to pool it seethed, leaped, splashed the mineral formations, proud in its opulence, intoxicated with bubbles, furious, foaming. His eyes filled with tears. Deafened by the tumult of the ceaselessly roaring torrent, he moved forward cautiously on to the slippery rock in the slim hope of weighing the emerald liquid in his hand. Hold water! Pathetic scrap of a man. No sooner had he skimmed it with his fingertips than he lost his footing. Then it was coming down on him with its full weight, sweeping him along in its depths with bursts of laughter. Gasping as the cold bit, Brice struggled against the current, but it was so strong that after a few seconds he gave up the fight. He felt strangely relieved, as if he had been waiting for this moment since birth. He was tired of fighting, tired of facing up. Perhaps this was where Emma was waiting for him. He needed only to let himself go. In a whirlpool his foot hit a stone and pain ripped him out of the kind of torpor in which he was sinking. His hand shot out of the foam and clutched a root.

Crouching on the corner of a rock, shaking, stupefied, he watched his hat swirling away to vanish on the glistening back of a waterfall, whose thundering waters plummeted a good ten metres on to jagged rocks beneath.

Shamefaced, teeth chattering, he limped back towards the village.

Luckily the chemist's shop was still open. Its green cross shone out against the rust-coloured sky. The pharmacist was busy attending to a customer. Taking in his pitiful state with one glance, she slipped out from behind the counter and rushed over to Brice.

'What on earth's happened to you, you poor man?'

'I fell, up by the spring. I must have sprained something.'

'I'll just finish serving this customer and I'll be right with you.'

Her gentle smile warmed his heart. He would have quite liked to call her 'Maman'. The pharmacy smelled clean, of toothpaste and safety. With a sigh of relief, he stretched out his injured leg. The customer in question was none other than the strange girl he had met at Martine's hair salon.

'This is the last time, Blanche. You must go back to the doctor's. I can't give you any more of your medication if you don't have a prescription. Do you understand?'

'Yes. Two packets.'

'No, Blanche. One, and then you come back with a prescription.'

'All right, one.'

Blanche's voice was, well, colourless, a wisp of a voice, barely audible, as if a ventriloquist were making her speak. As she was about to leave, she froze in front of Brice.

'What a waste of time.'

'I'm sorry?'

'I waited and waited.'

'You must be mistaken, I—'

'Come now, that's not kind. I've been worried. Well …'

She pursed her lips and shrugged, fiddling nervously with her little pearly purse. White stockings, white coat, white hat, white gloves. Only her eyes were black, as black as coal, almost aglow. Whipping a card from her pocket, she held it out with a feverish hand.

'Tomorrow, five o'clock, for tea.'

Without waiting for him to reply, she left the chemist's, as stiffly as a wooden soldier. The pharmacist crouched down in front of him. The gaping neck of her overall revealed two huge breasts, like the smooth rocks forming the mouth of the spring.

'That's quite a sprain you have there. I'll put some

ointment on and bandage it, but perhaps you should have it X-rayed as well.'

'All right. Tell me, who was that, the white lady?'

'Ah. Blanche Montéléger, from the big house on the edge of the village. She's a little … eccentric. I thought you knew each other.'

'No.'

'It's just that you look so much like her late father. I'm not hurting you, I hope?'

'No, not at all.'

The card was not printed but handwritten in curly old-fashioned script. No address or phone number, just *Blanche Montéléger*.

Emma and Brice had been arguing non-stop since the moment they woke up, about everything and, especially, about nothing. It was the first time this had happened to them and neither knew the reason for it now. Maybe it was because of the storm which was circling over the city without ever getting round to breaking. Every object seemed to be charged with electricity and made their hair stand on end as soon as they touched it.

'I've told you a hundred times to put the bread away in the basket. It dries out and gets thrown away, and I hate waste.'

'And you might change the toilet roll instead of leaving half a sheet.'

'The way you slam doors!'

'Could you turn the sound down? It's unbearable!'

Once they had exhausted their whole stock of petty

comments, each of them retreated into a stubborn silence which only increased their sense of unease. They paced around the flat like clockwork figures, brushing past each other in the corridors, avoiding looking at each other, ashamed, aware of the ridiculousness of the situation but unable to act normally. It was as if they had been replaced by grotesque doubles. It was a very difficult day, damp with sorrow, clouded by doubt, with that panicky fear of a child who has let go of its mother's hand. In the evening, when the storm finally broke, they fell into each other's arms. It had happened only once in ten years of marriage and yet this was the day he now found himself missing. How he would have loved to relive it, ten, a hundred, a thousand times!

Rolled up in his filthy sleeping bag on the creaky camp bed, amid the horrendous tip the garage had become, Brice felt like a boxer alone in the ring, up against himself. He needed to hit something, it didn't matter what. In spite of his swollen ankle he grabbed the five-kilo sledgehammer and headed for the kitchen. Emma had intended knocking down the wall between it and the dining room to make a kitchen-diner – far more sociable, she thought.

With the first blow, he felt as if the whole house were buckling at the knees and groaning, like an ox under the slaughterman's hammer. The impact reverberated through the shaft of the sledgehammer before spreading through him from head to foot. The vibrations went on for a good ten seconds. In the sink, a stack of plates collapsed. Horrified, he took in the terrible wound he had inflicted on the wall. Beneath the fragments of plaster, the pink flesh of the brick was visible and a long fissure ran from ceiling to floor. He had struck as hard as he could but the poor old wall was still standing. He had to finish it off. He gritted his teeth, closed his eyes and began pounding with all his might like a madman until, having hit empty space, carried along by the momentum of the tool, he circled on the spot like a hammer-thrower before collapsing on to the heap of rubble, wild-eyed and dazed. His ankle was swollen to twice its size. Plaster dust was gathering in his nose, making him want to throw up like after the first line of heroin. Without meaning to, he had created an almost perfectly circular hole through which the dining-room table and chairs could be seen, stock still and startled, like a flock whose rumination has been interrupted by a passing tourist. It was the first time he had knocked down a wall. His first wall ... He didn't know whether he should feel proud or sorry. He was tempted to turn himself in to the police. The house was sulking. Not one window would look him in the face.

It took him some time to clear up the rubble, and then he didn't know how to dispose of it. He filled ten bin bags and dotted them around the place like Easter eggs. Then he tried out the hole by going several times from kitchen to dining room and vice versa. It worked perfectly in both directions. Already he felt less guilty.

With a little bit of tidying up, it would be a very decent hole. The church clock struck four. Brice had a shower and ripped open a box marked 'Clothes' in order to extract something halfway suitable in which to visit Blanche Montéléger.

Never could Brice have imagined that the walking stick he had borrowed from the pharmacist would afford him so many pleasures. It was a perfectly ordinary one, however, with an ergonomic handle at one end and a rubber tip at the other. It helped him in his limping gait, of course, but in addition to this primary function it lent him the solemn elegance of a monarch who, by pointing the stick this way or that, kept the world at arm's length. It protected him from being too close to other people. He felt important. With a simple twirl of his stick he consigned this cruel, pathetic world to its humble fate, a billiard ball ricocheting around at the mercy of the void. Even as a child he had been fascinated by prosthetics. He would have liked to wear glasses or false teeth but unfortunately neither his eyes nor his gums had need of them. To make up for such tragic good health he had improvised glassless frames and stuck chewing gum over his teeth. As he neared thirty he really had needed glasses, and the dissolute life he led, consuming all sorts of illegal substances, got the better of his molars, canines and incisors. They had been replaced by metal, porcelain and resin. His wishes had been granted. Today, just as one is promoted to a higher rank, he had reached the age of the stick, the one before the apogee, the wheelchair. He aspired to this as might a candidate for a seat in the Académie française, a symbol of eternal rest and, heck, glory.

Even as he asked himself what his motive was for visiting Blanche Montéléger (curiosity? Nothing else to do?), he was amusing himself by trailing the end of his stick along the gates of people's houses in order to enrage the Alsatians, which would press their noses to the bars, causing a sort of riot as he went by. He loathed dogs, all dogs, for the good reason that they were man's best friend. In their dark cavernous mouths, foaming, and bristling with yellow fangs, and their eyes, which bulged from the pull of their chains, there was everything he hated in their masters.

The Montéléger house stood out dark against the sky like a regret. According to the pharmacist, it was the oldest in the village, the one from which all the rest had grown, developing like secondary tumours. It was completely surrounded by a wall built of Rhone pebbles in a chevron design. No light was coming from it. Beside a heavy grey wooden gate there was a battered letter box, above which there hung a sort of lavatory chain which gave a shrill sound when he pulled it. Once, twice, three times. He was about to turn on his heel when he heard footsteps on the other side of the oak panel.

The gate opened reluctantly, groaning for all it was worth, and Blanche appeared, wrapped in a blanket of indeterminate shade, throwing fearful glances over her shoulder.

'Are you alone?'

'Why ... yes.'

'Come in, quickly.'

She didn't so much walk as hop like a little mouse across the paved courtyard where a wreck of an ancient Citroën was rusting away. Brice had difficulty keeping up. As he moved forward, the front of the house seemed to lean over him, ready to crush him with the full weight of its shadow. A flight of steps took him to a door which Blanche asked him to come through swiftly. It was even darker and colder inside than out.

'I'm not putting the lights on because of the neighbours. People would talk. Give me your coat. Follow me.'

She was whispering so quietly he could barely hear her, and yet the slightest squeak of his shoe echoed round the vast hall like a gunshot. He followed her up a stone staircase and found himself in a huge room lit by one miserable bedside lamp on a stool, beside an armchair with a book left lying on it. A portable heater struggled valiantly to warm the atmosphere in front of an immense fireplace as cold as the mouth of a corpse. Contrary to what the splendid moulded ceiling might suggest, the room had the bare minimum of furnishings: a table, four chairs and a nondescript sideboard. No ornaments, no carpet, no paintings, not so much as a humble postcard pinned to the wall. Not a hint of imagination, not an ounce of femininity. Heavy curtains veiled the windows. The idiot of a blacksmith living in the church tower struck his anvil five times.

'You're on time. That's good.'

'It's difficult not to be, here. I admit I'm finding it hard to get used to that bell.'

'The church no longer has a priest; we need at least a bell to replace him. Do sit down.'

The tea was lukewarm and bitter, served in Duralex glasses, and the muffins that went with it were frankly disgusting.

'Do you like them? I baked them myself.'

'They're delicious.'

Blanche never stopped nervously intertwining her fingers. On close inspection she could be no more than thirty-five to forty. It was the way she expressed herself, choosing her words carefully, and the hesitation accompanying her every gesture which made her seem much older or much younger.

'A little more tea?'

'Please.'

Blanche seized objects as if they might escape her, and gripped them so tightly that her fingers turned white.

'How time passes. Do you think I've aged?'

'Er, I don't know.'

'I've aged, I know that. You, on the other hand, seem to have grown younger.'

'Listen, I think you're mistaken. You must be confusing me with someone else. I've only lived here for a month and I'd never been here before.'

'Ah. As you wish. Deep down, what does it matter? I know you, though. I have a very, very good memory. I remember everything!'

Brice didn't insist. Blanche seemed so certain that it made him doubt, and he told himself that, after all, the diaphanous little face was not entirely foreign. In the half-light of the room, it appeared to give off a glow like a night-light, the sort you place by the bedside of children afraid of the dark. Was it the lack of a familiar presence, something he suffered from more each day, which suggested this comparison to him? At all events, despite the strangeness of the place and situation, the pale aura emanating from her calmed him. She spoke softly, nibbling away at the silence. It was like the echo of his own solitude.

'When your foot recovers, the two of us will go for walks together.'

'I'd love that; I adore little country byways.'

'No. Along the main road. That's where you find things.'

'What sort of things?'

'Things. I'll show you.'

She disappeared momentarily into a pool of shadow at the back of the room and emerged carrying a heavy box.

'Look!'

With infinite care she took a pile of rubbish out of the box: assorted soft-drink cans, used tissues, cigarette packets, plastic bottles, tops, old rags, all squashed flat as if they'd been through a rolling mill.

'Here, have a look at this. What would you say it was?'

To Brice it was a grey-brown piece of dried mud with a zigzag on the top.

'It's a rat! A rat! I've got a toad as well. And—'

'That's … astonishing. And you pick all this up from the edge of the main road?'

'Every day. Ever since …'

A car had just drawn up in the courtyard. A door slammed. Blanche straightened up like a flick knife. Footsteps rang out on the staircase.

'Blanche? Blanche, it's me …'

A man of about seventy appeared, dressed in a khaki gamekeeper's uniform, with an oval brass badge saying 'La Loi' on his chest. He was dark and gnarled as if carved from a vine stalk.

'Oh, you've got company.'

'Come in, Élie, come in.'

Brice stood up, holding out his hand. The man hesitated for a moment, giving Blanche a strange look, before offering five tuber-like fingers.

'Brice Casadamont. I've just moved to Saint-Joseph, to the Loriol house.'

'Ah, yes.'

He immediately noticed Brice's swollen slippered foot.

'You're the one who fell at the waterfall?'

'Yes, unfortunately.'

'You shouldn't go there at this time of year.'

'I've learned my lesson. But it did allow me to make the acquaintance of Mademoiselle Blanche at the chemist's.'

'Right.'

This fortunate conjunction of events didn't seem to thrill him overmuch since he immediately looked away to speak to Blanche. 'I've brought the wood, three cubic metres. I'll leave it in the courtyard and put it away tomorrow.'

'Thank you, Élie. I was thinking of asking Monsieur to stay for dinner. Would you like to join us?'

'No, Blanche, not this evening. I've still got things to do. I'll put a basket of logs downstairs for you and cover the rest with a tarpaulin. It's going to rain. Good evening.'

And he was gone, ignoring Brice's hand. His steps could be heard dying away on the staircase, and then the door slammed. Blanche was holding her hands clasped in front of her chest and smiling.

'Élie's an old friend. A little brusque, but so devoted.'

'I don't doubt it.'

'You'll have dinner with me, won't you?'

'It's just … I wouldn't like to impose.'

'Oh do, please. I'll go and fetch the wood. We'll get a good fire going and I'll make the meal. Make yourself at home.'

'I'll help you.'

'You mustn't think of it with that foot. Sit down. You can light the fire.'

As he crumpled up some pages of a newspaper, he had time to read his horoscope, now three or four months out of date. 'Work: be adaptable, take the initiative. Love life: be adaptable, cover your back. Health: good.' Soon the fire was dancing merrily around the logs. The room looked like a fish tank in flames.

The packet soup was no more unpleasant than any other packet soup. As for the sardines in oil, worse had been known. The crackers were a bit soggy. Blanche kept up the conversation with the verbal incontinence of someone who hasn't spoken to another human since the world ended. Brice learned that she was thirty-nine, and the sole heir of an illustrious blue-blooded family; that her father Louis had finished squandering a fortune already significantly reduced by his ancestors and at his death, ten years earlier, had left her nothing but a mountain of debt. In order to keep the house she had had to sell everything, which explained the monastic look of the place. The small allowance she received for the chronic depression she had suffered since her beloved father's death enabled her to meet her modest needs.

'Your turn now. Tell me about yourself.'

'It's very simple. My wife and I wanted to move out of the city. She's a reporter; she travels a lot. In between trips she needs to rest. At the moment she's on an assignment abroad.'

'Ah. Abroad, that's a long way …'

Blanche looked at him in silence for a moment, with the intense stare of an Easter Island statue.

'You're waiting for your wife then?'

'Yes. I work as well, though. I'm a children's book illustrator.'

Blanche was no longer listening. She seemed to be stirring up the fire of her dark gaze. Nine o'clock struck.

'Nine o'clock! I'd better be going, I think. I've outstayed my welcome as it is.'

'This morning on the radio, an explorer just back from the South Pole was saying that the coasts down there are so polluted by what's thrown overboard from ships that birds build their nests from leftover bits of plastic, toothbrushes, combs, clothes pegs … That must be a sight worth seeing, don't you think?'

'Indeed. Well, thank you for the excellent dinner.'

'What?'

'Thank you for dinner.'

'Oh yes. It's raining. I'll lend you a brolly.'

They parted on the doorstep.

'Goodnight then, Blanche. It'll be my turn to invite you next time.'

'Yes. My father was an artist too, you know. He painted and wrote poems, really lovely ones. Goodbye.'

The sky was waterlogged, one immense pool.

Drifts of crumpled sketches were accumulating at Brice's feet. With every drawing, Sabine grew more and more hideous, more and more like Mabel Hirsch. For almost three hours now he had been pointlessly using up paper. It was because of the envelopes with windows (bank, electricity, taxes …), piles of which were reaching dangerous levels on the kitchen table, that he had got out his pencils, brushes, paper and inks that morning. The bottle of Chablis which he had expected to provide a modicum of inspiration now stood empty. He wasn't even drunk, just stultified, concreted up from the inside. He had two options: either he could slowly sink into the depths of the garage while he waited for Emma's return, or he could confront things and take the breaking wave of this life's sordid realities full in the face. The second of these was well beyond his capacities.

The less facing up he did, the less he wanted to do. Life was slipping through his fingers. That evening at Blanche's, for example, had entailed forty-eight hours' recovery time. Not because of an excess of food or drink, but because of the sudden closeness of another person in his emotional wilderness. Their hands had touched, she had smelled his scent and he hers, they had seen each other chewing and swallowing, laughed; she had noted the particular way he scratched the side of his nose, and he the way she was always twisting a lock of hair round her finger – a whole host of intimate revelations to which Brice was no longer accustomed. It was an offence to his solitude. Such closeness disgusted him. He consented to share it with Emma alone.

Emma wasn't jealous. He was, a little. When one of his exes phoned to find out how he was on the sly, she would make a point of exchanging a few polite words with her before handing him the receiver with a mischievous smile. When the boot was on the other foot, however, he would growl like a bear, holding out the phone as if it were a dirty sock. It had to be said that before him, poor Emma had gone out with a succession of guys each more stupid than the last. Especially Bob. That idiot of a photographer with his ludicrous action gilet covered in pockets, and travel anecdotes as boring as a show of holiday slides. Was he called Bob? He might have been.

All he felt good for was stuffing himself with crisps in front of the regional news on TV. Sweeping aside his drawing materials with his forearm, he stepped through the hole into the kitchen. In front of the fridge door, seated squarely on its bottom, tail neatly framing its paws, whiskers bristling, eyes bright and ears pricked up, a cat was looking at him with all the hauteur its little frame could muster. How had it got in? Brice was careful to check daily that all exits were sealed but the cat was well and truly there, as if it always had been. The look in its eyes was like that of Bombay beggars, disdainful and at the same time suffering. The creature yawned, revealing a pink chasm bristling with pointed teeth. It stretched out and then concertinaed in again before swaggering up to rub itself, purring, against his legs.

'The cat was created to give man the pleasure of stroking a tiger.' Brice had never wanted to stroke a tiger. He had never owned an animal, neither goldfish, canary nor tortoise. Only a solitary worm when he was aged fifteen. Animals, all of them, from the ant to the elephant, had always made him feel uneasy. He didn't understand them, nor they him. It was the same with people, but he had so far managed to survive among them thanks to the power of speech. The gift of the gab proved singularly ineffective with animals, unfortunately. The number of times he had got himself stung, bitten or scratched! Even so, on odd days when he felt down, he would find himself glued to a wildlife documentary showing lions devouring gazelles, giraffes giving birth, gnus getting stuck in mud and monkeys picking fleas off one another. But only because, on the other channels, people were slaughtering one another in increasingly horrible ways in dreadful American series. The cat persisted in wrapping itself round his legs, purring. Much too affectionate to be sincere. Food! Only food would get rid of it. Slowly he turned his upper body before taking one, then two steps towards the fridge and opening the door. He took out a bottle of milk and poured a little into a saucer. Even before he had put it on the floor, the cat was upon it. It was as simple as that. Now all he had to do was find the poison ...

Was it a male or a female cat? Brice bent down but it was impossible to see beneath the tufts of fur. The creature was lapping greedily, and when it had finished it gave him a grateful look which threw him completely. He allowed the animal to climb on to his lap and rub its cuddly head against his tummy. His hand began to move back and forth on the silky coat.

'Who are you then? Where've you come from? Boy or girl?'

Impassive, almost solemn, the cat was kneading his thighs. Really, the nature of its sex had no more significance than that of angels. As for how it had got into the heart of his private world, that was its own affair. He would never have thought that stroking a cat would be so agreeable. He could have gone on for hours, breathing to its rhythm, not moving. But a tractor passing in the street made the cat's ears prick up, and it leaped from his lap to disappear off somewhere only it knew. Already Brice was missing it. He opened a tin of sardines and ate half, putting the rest out for the cat in the hope it would come back. He so much needed to be one of a pair.

He didn't immediately recognise the ring of the doorbell, for the simple reason that until now no one had visited him. Only at the second attempt did he realise that the call was intended for him. He shot up from his camp bed, sending the sleeping cat off his tummy and into a box of glassware he had opened that morning in search of a Thermos.

'Hello, Blanche.'

'Good evening. I've brought you some soup.'

'But ... That's very kind. Do come in.'

Brice led her into the dining room and sat her down while he cleared a heap of rubbish from the table. To his great shame he noticed the room smelled like a tip.

'Please excuse me. I'm in the middle of some work.'

'I can see. That hole's big.'

'I'm going to make a kitchen-diner; my wife prefers it. Tea?'

'Yes, please. Ah, you've a cat?'

The cat, which Brice had encountered again that morning, faithful to its post in front of the fridge, had not left his side all day. Now it was prowling around Blanche, arching its back and rubbing against her fur-lined ankle boots.

'I love cats. Here, kitty … come and sit on my knee. What's its name?'

'I don't know. I found it here the other day. I don't even know how it gets in and out.'

'I used to have one long ago, Pompon, but then it died. We shouldn't grow attached … It just means sorrow afterwards.'

On her knee, the cat luxuriated in her caresses, while Blanche swept the walls and ceiling with her gaze, smiling. The kitchen's cataclysmic appearance seemed not to surprise her in the least.

'It's a beautiful house.'

'It will be. There's still a lot to do.'

'Your wife is lucky to have such a considerate husband.'

Blanche's smile had gone. A shadow crossed her face but gave way immediately to the opalescent luminosity which served her as make-up.

'It's pea and lardon soup. Do you like that?'

'I love it. I must confess I don't do much cooking at the moment.'

'It's very easy to make, you know. I bought four packets for the price of one. All you do is add water and stir and …'

She was making the gesture with her hand, as if to convey to him that the whole secret of the recipe lay in this rotating motion of the wrist. He watched her, unable to take his eyes off the invisible spoon which was turning.

Emma could make only one thing, béchamel sauce. She never got it wrong. The wooden spatula would make a spiral in the sauce, which thickened little by little into an unctuous cream. Emma, Emma, Emma …

'… otherwise it goes lumpy.'

'Sorry?'

'Otherwise it goes lumpy. Aren't you feeling well?'

'I'm perfectly fine, thank you.'

'That's good. If I may … I've brought you a little poem by my father. Would you like to read it?'

'With pleasure.'

From her purse she drew a piece of paper folded in eight and, unfolding it with the greatest of care, handed it to him with a blush.

A Father's Oath

Beautiful child, you make my life worthwhile.
Light grey eyes and pinkly budding smile.
A nose as small's a button, tiny ears.
Ne'er will I fail to wipe away your tears.
Companion on life's steep, mysterious ways,
How, without you, could I get through my days?
Ever a father's love will with you go.

Let it protect and guide you, teach and show.
Only one girl is ruler of my heart,
Uniquely you, with whom I'll never part.
If you read this carefully,
See how close we'll always be.

Carefully, Brice refolded the yellowing sheet and gave it back to Blanche. 'He was a witty man, your father.'

'Oh yes, he was great fun to be with.'

'And your mother?'

'I hardly knew her. I lost her when I was very young.'

'I'm sorry.'

'Why? I never missed her.'

Blanche lifted the cat which was purring on her knee and placed it delicately on the floor.

'A little more tea?'

'No, thank you. I must be getting back. About the soup, heat it gently. You mustn't boil it or it'll thicken and won't be so nice.'

'Absolutely. Would you like your Tupperware back?'

'Another time. Take care of your foot. We can look forward to some lovely walks together; good weather's forecast.'

'I'm keen to make the most of it. Well, thank you for coming, and for the soup. I sense I have a feast in store.'

'It's nothing. Oh, you should put curtains at your window. In a village you always need good thick curtains. A window without curtains is like an eye without an eyelid.'

'I'll do that. I promise.'

A gust of wind took advantage of Blanche's exit to rush into the house and have a look around, ruffling a napkin, a newspaper, a fluff ball and the cat's whiskers as it went by, before it disappeared up the chimney, sniggering.

'Look, Dominique, I'll be honest with you. I no longer give a toss about Mabel Hirsch, or Sabine, or you, or the money, or my career. I've had it up to here with that shit.'

'OK, Brice, OK. We'll manage. Please, take care of yourself. Don't hesitate to ring me if there's anything at all you need.'

'What I need is for people to bloody well leave me in peace!'

The telephone let out a pathetic whimper as he slammed it back on the table. He was angry with himself immediately. None of this was its fault, poor thing. It had done its job. But things, oh the things! Hundreds and thousands of them were swarming around him in the shadows of the garage. Boxes spewed out new ones every day. Each one of them was waiting for him to give it a function, a job, and all he could do was scatter them around haphazardly, forcing them into a sort of monstrous orgy. Of course they ended up mating, engendering the inconceivable. It was hard to imagine the love child of a vegetable mill and a pair of skis. It was horrendous, like being in a Hieronymus Bosch painting.

Only the cat seemed able to find its way in the shambles. It would prowl around, sniffing, nimbly dodging a precariously balanced lampshade to sprawl on a rolled-up anorak, knead a silk rug with its claws, juggle with a table-tennis ball, get tangled up in a cotton reel. It was enchanted by this joyous disorder.

Brice, on the other hand, sat with his elbows on the camping table in the cone of light from the bedside lamp, searching desperately for a sense to it all. The radio was telling him that the world's smallest dog measured 17 centimetres and weighed 850 grams, and that in Africa, 1 in 16 women died before the age of thirty, while in Europe it was only 1 in 36,000. The stock market was holding up pretty well. The hunters were angry and so were the motorcyclists, but not for the same reason. A bomb in a cemetery had killed 112 people, with 2 missing. Close study of eel movement suggested it might one day be possible for a submarine to make a 45-degree turn at a speed of …

Just as the two jaws of the vice gripping his skull were about to meet, he switched off the transistor. The ensuing silence made him feel as if he had plunged his head underwater. Then suddenly there was a strange sound, as if from beyond the grave, like a heart beginning to beat again in the chest of a corpse. A single note, a mi perhaps, or a soh. Having just knocked down the guitar case, the cat sought refuge between his legs, its fur standing on end.

Every man in his fifties has a guitar slumbering in his house. That lost chord came from so far away! Brice opened the case with as much care as an Egyptologist a sarcophagus. In its red velvet casket, the Gibson's silky wood positively glowed. Only the strings seemed a little rusty. The guitar was as light as a young bride when he rested it on his thigh. Barely out of tune. With the middle finger of his left hand he played the harmonics. As good as new. The wide-eyed cat could not believe the way the man's fingers were making the piece of furniture sing. It leaped on to the table and tried to bite the steel whiskers sticking out of the tuning pegs, which were like its own.

Brice had bought it second-hand in Pigalle, a real bargain, with the money from his first contract. He had been dreaming of it for years.

One day he had tried to impress Emma by playing her a very complicated piece. As he hadn't practised for quite a long time, however, his fingers had got mixed up and Emma had burst out laughing. Annoyed, he had shut the instrument away in its case and never opened it again.

Delicately Brice laid the instrument back in its coffin.

'Grief is something you learn, Brice. Dr Boaert is a great help to us, and he's willing to see you.'

'Not me.'

'You have to get help. She's dead, the consulate itself …'

'To hell with the consulate and Dr Boaert. Her body hasn't been found. You know what that is, a body? A thing with two arms, two legs and sometimes a head. Until I've seen it with my own eyes, I won't believe it, and even—'

'Calm down, young Brice.'

'Myriam, you're very kind, but do stop calling me "young Brice". There's only a handful of years between us.'

'We're only trying to help you!'

'I don't need help! I just want to be bloody well left in peace!'

Brice heard a muffled sob and, in the background, Simon's discordant voice.

'I'm sorry, Myriam. I'm a little tired. Could you put Simon on, please?'

'Yes, just a second …'

'Hello, Brice. Simon here.'

'Hi, Simon. You mustn't be cross with me. I know you're fond of me, and I am of you, but I swear I don't need anyone. Do you understand?'

'Yes, Brice. But Myriam's a mother, so …'

His voice was barely audible. He had never raised it in his life. The telephone must have been trembling in his hand. Forty years with the railways. A fishing rod and an alarm clock as retirement gifts, an attractive stone villa on the banks of the Saône, with a never-ending sunset as a backdrop …

'Simon, you mustn't worry about me. I'm getting on fine – at least, I'm getting on. I promise I won't hesitate to phone if I need anything. But not just yet, not …'

'Of course, Brice. I understand … What's the weather like with you?'

'Dreary. It's drizzling but according to the radio it should improve in the coming week.'

'Ah, that's good. It's not all blue skies here either; it's foggy, damp.'

'Are you catching fish?'

'A few whitebait, but Myriam doesn't like them so I throw them back in the water.'

'We'll have a fine trip one of these days, OK?'

'OK. Right, well, we'll let you get on, Brice. All the best!'

'You too, Simon. Give Myriam a kiss from me.'

The way men talk to each other, with their pathetic little meaningless words and all that space between the lines …

The cat was asleep on his lap, or pretending to be. It was like a loaf fresh from the oven, so warm and round and solid. A burning smell reached his nostrils.

'Shit, the potatoes!'

Because of that bloody phone call, Brice already regretted having invited his neighbour to dinner. Why did they all persist in building a future for him? He was sick of the lot of them! He had made a blanquette. That was a dish he usually managed not too badly. In the nick of time he rescued the potatoes by running them under the tap. The rest just needed to be heated up. Blanquette was always better reheated. He had started preparing it first thing that morning.

This was the dish which had helped him win Emma. She had loved it; they'd eaten it for two days. What was Emma eating now?

The wooden spoon slipped from his fingers. He felt irresistibly drawn to the plughole. He would have loved to dissolve, to disappear through the little holes and join her somewhere in the labyrinth of waste pipes, since that is where the dead live, down below.

He held his hands under the tap for a long time as if trying to wash away the traces of some unknowable crime. 'Set the table. I've got to set the table. Place mats, where are the place mats?'

He had chanced on them the day before while looking for clean underpants. He thought he remembered roughly where they were. As he trod on the first step leading down to the garage, he stumbled on an object he had never come across before: a gilt metal bust, fairly heavy and some twenty centimetres high, of Camillo (his name was engraved on it), the unforgettable voice behind 'Sag Warum'. What was the old fool doing there? Emma must have unearthed him in a junk shop for kitsch. Camillo … 'Sag Warum' … Straight away, the sleeve of the 45 which had got a generation dancing and flirting came back to him: a sad-looking, wiry-haired old charmer wreathed in smoke. The oh-so slow number they had been crazy about at the youth club in Porchefontaine. There was the bar covered in bamboo, the tartan lampshade perched on a Vat 69 bottle, the red lights … A *poc-poc* sound could be heard from the next room, where boys too spotty to have a hope of getting lucky were taking out their frustrations at the ping-pong table. Everyone swigged Orangina while the girls wiggled about to 'La Bamba'.

Afterwards they would go home on foot, or riding two to a moped, a Peugeot BB or a Flandria.

*

Whose past was this, rising in his throat with the acid juices of a bad hangover? What if all this was some huge con, designed to give him the illusion that he was alive? These memories might well have been crammed into his head when he was asleep, along with the date of the Battle of Marignano (1515), nine nines are eighty-one, words spelt with a circumflex accent, man's first steps on the moon. What proof did he have of all that? And Mabel Hirsch, Dominique Porte, Myriam, Simon, even Emma! Nothing could be taken for granted. And wasn't Blanche Montéléger a kind of mirage as well? Might not the fronts of the buildings in his street be held up by wooden props like on a film set, lasting for one take? Just one take …

Only the bust of Camillo seemed substantial, because of its weight. He took it back up to the dining room and placed it in the centre of the table.

'Your Beethoven is handsome.'

'That's not Beethoven; it's Camillo.'

'Ah. He's still handsome.'

'Can I give you some more, Blanche?'

'No, thank you. It was very good.'

'A little salad with the cheese, then.'

Brice was having trouble standing, yet he had drunk only two or three glasses of an excellent wine Blanche had brought, a bottle which had escaped her father's ruin. A black film appeared before his eyes while he was tossing the salad. He had to clutch the edge of the sink with both hands to stay on his feet. On the outside of the salad bowl he could see the curved reflection of Blanche behind him, eyes glued to the bust of the Teutonic crooner. During the meal they had exchanged only small talk. However, the pleasantries seemed gradually to take on a double meaning. By the time he had deciphered the hidden one, he had forgotten the first, with the result that he was always a beat behind in the conversation. Yet he wasn't drunk; he was in fact terribly lucid. He turned the tap full on and splashed his face with ice-cold water.

'Don't you feel well?'

'I'm fine. I suddenly felt hot, that's all.'

'Perhaps it's the wine.'

'Perhaps. Do excuse me. Here's the salad. Now, there's Picodon, and some Etorki—'

'Is your wife coming back soon?'

'I'm sorry? Oh, Emma. Yes, very soon. Camembert and—'

'Where did you say she was?'

'In Egypt.'

'That's a long way away.'

'Er, yes. And Comté—'

'I wouldn't like to go so far away. I'd be afraid I wouldn't find my way back again.'

He was no longer in control of the cheeseboard. Everything became soft, blurred, opaque.

The tiled floor was cool and yielding; his body was sinking into it. The Picodon rolled along the skirting board, the portion of Etorki was pointing towards his ear like the prow of a ship, and the Camembert came to a halt beneath a chair. Above him, two feet began dancing a peculiar jig and then there was nothing but a long fade to black.

*

A limp piece of seaweed felt cool on his brow. Blanche had prominent cheekbones and unbelievably red lips, and as for her teeth! Almost as many as she had fingers – at least thirty.

'Can you hear me? Can you hear me?'

Of course he could hear her. Her mouth was ten centimetres from his nose. The ceiling beams seemed dangerously bowed. It was as if they were bearing some enormous weight: the whole sky, maybe.

'What are you saying?'

'Nothing. I didn't say anything.'

'Are you feeling better?'

'I don't know. I feel a bit cold.'

As he propped himself up on one elbow, the whole world tipped sideways. The damp towel on his forehead fell on to his face. He took it off to find himself nose to nose with the cat, which was sniffing him in a battle of whiskers.

Returning to a vertical position was a delicate operation. The chair he managed to get on to appeared bony but solid.

'I think I was taken ill, wasn't I?'

'These things happen.'

'I'm so sorry.'

'I'm used to it. My father often fell down like that. He liked to drink.'

'But I didn't have anything to drink apart from the two or three glasses of wine with the meal.'

'In that case it's the solitude that doesn't agree with you.'

Blanche was every inch the nurse who saves the hero in a bad war film, wearing her heart on her sleeve and an indelible smile.

'Well, if you're feeling better, I'm going to go. It's getting late.'

Blanche slipped her coat on. It gave off a disturbing scent of nothingness, the same odour which had struck him on his arrival in the house: the inimitable perfume of emptiness.

'Hang on a second, Blanche. Take the statuette.'

'Is it a present?'

'Yes.'

She took it in her hands like a relic, and teardrops appeared in the corners of her eyes.

'It's heavy. I'll give it a good clean. Is it gold?'

'I don't think so.'

'Oh, it is, it's gold! Thank you!'

'The toothbrush doesn't go there; it goes here!'

For some time now he had been in the habit of talking to himself. Depending on his mood, he would concoct domestic squabbles for himself, or little compliments. If you have an inner life you inevitably have a double life. It remained to be seen which of the two lives would gobble up the other. The funny turn he had had during the dinner with Blanche had seriously thrown him. Even if nothing like it had happened since, he remained on the alert nonetheless. The sense that his self had been taken from him impelled him to cling to the slightest of his memories so as to keep himself together. He had to admit, however, that doubts were swarming inside him like worms in a fruit. He was about to brush his teeth when, in the bathroom mirror, he discovered with amazement that he had a beard. And not two days' growth, either. A proper beard! A good three centimetres of salt-and-pepper bristles covering his cheeks, chin and upper lip. How had that grown in one night? Unless he had lost sight of himself some time ago?

It was Sunday then. The bell was going full swing. Getting through Sunday was a lengthy business, very lengthy.

How many of them had he lived through? Hundreds, thousands, all identical, those interminable Sundays which, from earliest childhood, inure us to boredom as to a drug. The morning was all right: there was the market, the smell of roast chicken drifting through the house, the clouds of eau de Cologne from the bathroom where, for once, everyone had been able to take their time. The midday meal was a sort of Christmas dinner. But, winter or summer, by three o'clock it was as sombre as All Saints' Day. If you were not snoring, hands on belly, in front of the TV which was going round like a washing-machine drum, then you would go down to meet your mates in the car park, a football tucked under your arm. The older you became, the less use you made of the ball. It was taken for a walk like a faithful old dog. Sitting on a low concrete wall, you would roll it around distractedly beneath your foot while you played, 'What would you do if you won the lottery?' Unlike their fathers who had always played it safe, putting their money on houses, cars, dogs and wives, their dreams still had a certain class: pilot (any sort), pop star, adventurer. Everyone knew it was wrong to aspire to a different future from the one their parents had in mind for them: engineer (any sort), civil servant, lawyer, doctor. But time was still on their side.

There was an unbelievable number of beer caps stuck into the tarmac, a Kronenbourg galaxy amid which the ball was kicked haphazardly back and forth. Later, when the streetlights came on and the sky imitated the car park, everyone went home. Sometimes the ball was left behind. After the big film, Monday was as good as there.

His ankle needed exercise. Ten chimes rang out crystal clear on the pure air. He put on his coat, picked up his stick and found himself in the street, breathing in big lungfuls of fresh woodsmoke-scented air. He stopped in front of the cemetery, which seemed a good place to extend his acquaintance with the locals. He pushed open the gate which failed to creak mournfully. It looked like a walled garden with cypress trees, bushy hedges, benches, and even the odd tomb to justify the nature of the place. People here didn't die much. A small Sacred Heart for the Cahusset family, local dignitaries no doubt; a half-dozen or so marble plaques in varying states of upkeep; and three or four molehills with lopsided crosses on the top. A concrete slab, recent in appearance and covered in a riot of fresh flowers, had as its centrepiece the childlike smile of a young man of around twenty who had, according to the gilded inscription, fallen victim to a man-eating plane tree while minding his own business doing 180 kph on his motorbike on the main road.

Between two cypresses he came upon the Montéléger vault. Engraved on the grey stone were a host of Clothères, Mariuses, Anselmes and Victors, and their wives, Suzannes, Marie-Louises, Fernandes and Marthes, all Montélégers. Most of the sepia photographs depicting them in their glory days were, because of the mist which had formed under their glass domes, now mere ghosts, vague outlines, auras of life on the point of definitive extinction. The most recent, depicting Louis, was by contrast absolutely clear. To judge by the dates, this had to be Blanche's father. He was smiling behind his beard, but awkwardly, as if under constraint. His weary expression was not without similarity to the one which had looked back at Brice in the bathroom mirror that morning. Perhaps it was because of his sudden beard, but there was an indefinable family resemblance between this Louis and him. When he stood up again, he found a small bunch of freshly picked white flowers.

They had no smell, or rather they smelled of Blanche's coat. Brice continued to crunch his way along the gravel paths, and a little further on flopped on to a bench, arms and legs outstretched, his face upturned to the gentle rays of the sun. He dozed off for a moment. In front of him the gravestones pitched like leaky old tubs gone aground in the Bay of Douarnenez.

A bee came and settled by his hand on the back of the bench. An old bee, swamped by its oversized yellow and black striped jacket. It must have come a long way, from the previous summer maybe. It could go on no longer, panting and waggling its antennae as if trying to pick up Radio London. It began turning round and round on the spot, frantically waving its spindly legs: 'Where d'you go to die around here?' In one last effort, it vibrated its wings but managed only a fatal loop-the-loop which threw it over on its back. Brice thought of shortening its sufferings with a well-aimed blow from his walking stick, but against all expectations it righted itself again and directed a still formidable sting at his hand, before taking off once more on its wandering flight towards the backstage area of life, where no audience member is allowed to enter.

It was a tiny scrap of paper folded into quarters, found deep in a pocket, a poem of the everyday.

Leeks, parsley, lemon
Drain unblocker
Bread
Milk, instant mash
Ham
Pot scourer
Shoes from repairer's

Between the lines of this short list of errands, the watermark of a whole day became visible, an ordinary yet unique day which flitted past Brice's eyes in its entirety, in a fraction of a second.

He and Emma had woken up furry-mouthed. The evening with the Planchons had been long and seriously liquid. While making the coffee he noticed that the sink was still blocked. An enormous pile of washing-up stood on the draining board. The Scotch-Brite scourer was on its last legs, both sides in shreds.

'Let's have something light to eat this evening.'

'Ham and mash?'

'Perfect!'

'I'll make a list.'

'Oh, could you pick up my shoes from the repairer's? Ugh, this coffee's disgusting! Oh God, my head's killing me … See you this evening, darling. Have a good day.'

When he came back from shopping, he unblocked the sink and did the washing-up while listening to the radio. A psychologist was explaining that eight people in ten wished to change their lives. Oddly enough, though, when asked to be specific about the life they dreamed of, what they described was almost exactly the life they had been leading all day every day since birth. Emma's shoes smelled of glue. If he had not found that scrap of paper he might not have remembered that day. How many others had he lived that had since melted away into oblivion?

The camp bed groaned as he stood up. He kicked it, hard. He was in no mood to listen to its tales of woe.

Sensing the atmosphere, the cat crept under a quilt at the other end of the garage, wisely deciding this was not the moment to claim its meagre rations. The weather was neither good nor bad; there was only a blank sky like a blind man's eyes. Brice felt stiff and weak. His body needed to move about, loosen up a bit. He decided to go to the chapel he could see from his window, at the very top of the hill. He didn't even think about his ankle as he strode up the slope. His walking stick whipped the brambles mercilessly. A drum was pounding in his chest, cymbals clanging in his ears. Snails braked sharply as his heavy shoes crossed their paths.

His anger kept him going at the same furious pace until the top of the hill, but as he reached the threshold of the chapel he collapsed in a heap, red-faced and short of breath. Seen from a distance through binoculars, the chapel appeared larger than it was. Never could a donkey, an ox and a family of Palestinian émigrés have fitted inside at the same time. Besides, there was no longer any roof, or a cross, only the façade to deceive you. The whole sky was visible through it. He lay flat against the stone slabs with his mouth wide open. He felt the urge to graffiti that stupid blank sky, to spray-paint, 'Piss off, the lot of you'. Not a trace of the divine, damn all, nada.

There was a smell of damp earth, mossy stone, mushrooms. His right hand skimmed a clump of heather. It was soft. The first time he had put his hand in a girl's knickers had been at the Kursaal, his local cinema. *The Ten Commandments*, three hours of film. That was how long it took to achieve your ends in those days. Just as old Moses was parting the Red Sea with his staff, Brice had managed to get his finger in Sylvie's pussy. The Promised Land was no longer terra incognita.

He wiped his penis with a tissue. The heather was barely ruffled.

'Not many people like Viandox.'

Blanche was stitching an Alsatian's head on a canvas. It was freezing in the room; the electric heater was not plugged in and there was no flame dancing in the grate. Brice was warming his numb fingers round the cup of boiling-hot beef stock.

'Do you like dogs, Blanche?'

'No, they smell. Martine gave me this design; her mother has a needlework shop. From time to time she gives me them because she knows I love embroidery. I've already done one of Claude François in a disco outfit, and a peasant scene. The problem is I don't always have the right colour wool. It's kind of you to come and see me.'

'I was on my way down from the chapel and since I was passing, I thought …'

'You did the right thing. Do you see how good your Camillo looks on the mantelpiece?'

Beneath his bushy eyebrows, the crooner surveyed the frozen wastes of the living room.

'He looks far better here than in my house.'

Sitting by the window in the half-light like a girl in a Flemish painting, Blanche suddenly stopped moving her needle to and fro.

'I wanted to ask you …'

'Do, please …'

'Could I come and watch television at your house tomorrow morning?'

'But … Of course.'

'I noticed the other night that you own one. My father didn't like television. He used to say it made people stupid. But I'm very fond of television. I'm not afraid of being stupid. I'll be there at half past eight. Martine's told me about a programme where they show you things.'

'All right then, eight-thirty tomorrow.'

'That's very kind. Would you mind lighting the fire?'

'Not at all, I'd be glad to.'

In the fireplace Brice heaped an armful of vine stalks, which caught light straight away, and then he placed two fine oak logs on top. In winter, there is something reassuring about hell.

'That Alsatian's very handsome, Blanche, especially with its red eye.'

'I had no blue left.'

The fire crackled. Crouching in front of the hearth, he bathed his hands in the warmth of the flames. For the first time in ages he felt at home, as if he had always belonged here. They stayed like that, in wordless intimacy, until a log slipped as the bell rang for half past seven.

'Tomorrow evening Élie's releasing pheasants. Do you feel like coming?'

'Releasing pheasants?'

'For shooting. They call them surprise releases. Around one hundred cocks and hens. It's a wonderful sight. The crates are opened and the birds take flight, flapping their wings. You'd think they were applauding.'

'Applauding what?'

'I don't know. Freedom ... their impending death ... Who knows why people applaud? Élie could tell you the whereabouts of every last fox and badger den, the quails' nests, coypu burrows in the riverbank, the hiding places of perch, eels and carp. All the secrets ... in holes ...'

Blanche had put down her needlework. The dog's head was hanging over her knees. She stared into the fire. A deep furrow lined her brow.

'What's the use of taking short cuts if you're going nowhere? What's the point of going away, leaving those you love? Why do they all go away? They *know* they'll hurt us, so why d'they do it? Go and hide in their dirty dark holes. They chuck us away like cast-offs ... They'll never come back, never!'

With these last words she had stood up so abruptly that her chair toppled over, scraping against the floor. Brice reached towards her shoulder but thought better of touching it for fear of electrocution. It was like being near an exposed wire. For several long minutes the room seemed alive with electricity. Then the church bell shook the walls eight times, and Blanche relaxed.

'Blanche, can I do anything for you?'

'I'm sorry?'

'Would you like me to call a doctor?'

'For what?'

'You seem so ... nervous.'

'It's nothing. It happens to me sometimes ... Forgive me, I'm tired.'

'I'll leave you then. See you tomorrow at half past eight, for your programme.'

'Oh yes, the programme ... Yes, of course. Good-night.'

He went home feeling he had narrowly escaped being struck by lightning, yet already with a sense of loss.

Élie's van smelled of scrap metal, engine grease, chicken shit and other rotting organic matter. In the back, Blanche and Brice were being jolted about like parachutists in an aircraft cabin, seated opposite each other, he on a tyre, she on a heap of grey blankets. Blanche looked in seventh heaven. The angels were shut up in groups of four inside a dozen perforated crates from which occasional rustling of feathers and muffled clucking could be heard. Three hens and one cock pheasant to a crate.

Élie had not seemed exactly thrilled to have Brice there too, but had nonetheless offered him the tool which served him as a hand, while trading pointed glances with Blanche. The light was fading gently above the hills. All that could be seen was lavender blue, and purple streaks in a weary sky. Turning off into a side track, the van stopped at the edge of a field of maize. The noise of its sliding door was like a guillotine. Blanche leaped out, alert and fresh as a trout, while Brice struggled to extricate himself from his tyre under Élie's mocking gaze. The gamekeeper took out a crate and set it down at the edge of the field.

'Blanche, come and do the honours.'

'No, Brice and I will do it together. Come on, it's very simple. You undo the wire hooks and ... Are you ready?'

The inside of the crate was humming like the wings of a theatre before curtain up.

'I'm ready.'

'One, two, three.'

Once the lid was lifted, the birds burst out, the deafening beating of their wings sounding more like slaps than applause. In a split second, at a height of three metres, each of them chose its direction, some opting for the forest, some the field, others the main road. One of them refused to leave the crate and had to be persuaded with a kick. A fraction of a second to choose your destiny, or rather the place where the huntsman would put an end to it, forest, field, main road ... The one which had refused to come out of the crate, a splendid cock, settled a few metres away by the roadside, resigned. Élie aimed a clod of earth at it. Brice heard him mutter right beside him, 'It's not just the cocks that should clear off.'

Blanche was clapping her hands, looking at the sky

which, as per usual, appeared to have no interest in anything.

'Another, Élie, one more …'

They released others up on the crest, among the vines, along the edge of the motorway. Brice held some in his hands, felt their hearts swell at the call of a freedom they had never demanded, since they were all bred in captivity. His hair and beard were flocked with grey down. All the crates were empty now, but it was as if a pulse were still beating there. Darkness had gathered in the back of the van. Only the oval of Blanche's face could be seen, like a veiled moon. She was wearing the same beatific smile as that morning in front of the TV.

She had rung the doorbell at eight-thirty on the dot. He had just had time to pull on trousers and a shapeless sweater and open the door, bleary-eyed, with wisps of dreams floating round his head.

'Has it started?'

'I don't know. Do come in.'

She followed him into the dim maze of the garage and sat down on the edge of the camp bed, knees together, twisting an invisible handkerchief between her fingers, like a little girl on her first visit to the cinema.

'It's on Channel One, you said?'

'Yes.'

'That's lucky. The reception's bad on the others.'

With a little adjustment to the aerial, the picture

settled down. A couple of presenters – the male component being a former weather man in a new toupee – were in a show house, brimming over with enthusiasm about a batch of non-stick film, available either in rolls measuring 40 x 33 centimetres or in 33-, 26- or 24-centimetre discs, to protect the base of your saucepans or baking trays for eternity, for the modest sum of €24.95. Blanche could not believe her eyes.

'I'm going to make some coffee. Would you like some?'

'No, thank you, I've already had my hot chocolate. Did you see that? Only €24.95 for eternity!'

Brice no longer had the heart to make himself real coffee, making do with a jar of instant. He carried his bowl back in and sipped it next to Blanche, who applauded at the appearance of each new product. A 72-piece canteen containing twelve sets of top-quality gilt stainless-steel cutlery for €59.95 – that's right, just €59.95! The must-have laser level in sturdy carry case, for €79.95. The protein-enriched instant rejuvenating cream that fights dark circles and puffiness, endorsed by a showbiz veteran wheeled out for the occasion, at €29.95 a jar. The multi-purpose, natural, ecological, hypo-allergenic cleaning product that makes everything look like new, from the children's dirty trainers to your copper pans or the inside of the fridge, for €14.95. The unmissable 250-watt juicer with two-year guarantee, for great vitamin-packed breakfasts, at €151.95. And the famous massage cushion covered in little electric fingers to tickle you from head to toe, at €69.95 …

Blanche marvelled at all these wondrous inventions, and Brice ended up getting into the spirit as well. When it came down to it, the programme was no more stupid than a political debate, or a documentary on coelacanths or the arduous life of a clogmaker in the Ardèche. TV was TV. It was not what it showed you that mattered but the way you looked at it, like the ever-changing patterns of a kaleidoscope. It could still be watched when it was switched off.

Lolling on the bed like a twist of soft marshmallow, he felt comfortable beside Blanche. It reminded him of childhood days when he was kept at home with a cold or touch of flu. The bedroom smelled of herbal tea and suppositories. The thermometer struggled to reach 38.2°C; comics lay strewn over the bed. He didn't really feel unwell; he just had no desire to do anything. From the kitchen came the sound of saucepans, wafts of bouillon, and his mother's voice humming along to a tune on the radio. It was like being alive and yet dead, a phantom who could go through walls, infiltrating the domestic intimacy of the woman busy at the stove. Even his father had no access there. Very early on he had developed a liking for these benign illnesses. He had contracted them all, from catarrh to hand, foot and mouth disease. He would happily have spent the holidays in a coma.

Blanche gave off a scent of plain, honest Marseilles soap. Her hip was touching his and their calves brushed occasionally, but he felt no physical desire. They were quite simply where they needed to be at that precise moment. But the clock struck the half-hour and Téléachat came to an end.

Blanche gave a sigh. 'That was good, wasn't it?'

'Very good.'

'All those inventions, just to make life easier for us. People don't take care of things any more. They throw them away as soon as they get tired of them. Listen, I know a lovely graveyard for objects. It's huge. Would you like to go there?'

'When?'

'Now. It's not far but we'll still need to take the car. It's a real goldmine, you know!'

'Well … Why not? I'll just get dressed and then we'll go.'

The rubbish tip looked like Stromboli, Etna, any one of the world's volcanoes, a sort of cut-off pyramid wrapped in steam and gases. After parking the car, they had to wade through a greasy black mire bristling with pieces of scrap metal, wooden beams and shards of glass, in order to reach the crater where they dispersed a colony of gulls and crows poking about with their beaks amid swirls of grey smoke. There was a smell of rotten cabbage, compost, the 'after' coming into being.

A colossal pile of shit. The earth, or rather the sticky mush that made every movement difficult, seemed eager to absorb them at every step, to gobble, suck and digest and then spit them out again, waste among waste, for its sole function was to consume to the point of revulsion. Despite the aid of his stick Brice several times almost went under. He was covered in mud up to his knees, while Blanche hopped here and there, spotless, like the gulls.

'Look, come and see how beautiful it is!'

The ancient fridge with its rounded corners lay half buried in the mud, its gaping door offering a rust-flecked shelter to the weary sky.

'People chose this, one day, in a department store.'

'A young couple, with no children, because it's not very big. A wedding present perhaps?'

'That's it! They took it home to their small apartment … They were happy.'

'Probably.'

'What's become of them?'

Blanche suddenly dissolved into tears and began scrabbling around in the mud with both hands, like a madwoman.

'Stop that, Blanche. You might hurt yourself. There's all sorts of nasty things in there.'

'This earth that takes everything away from us and gives us nothing in return!'

She stood up again, shaking with anger, and threw a fistful of mud at a gull, which flew off with a squawk.

Wiping her nose with the back of her hand, she inadvertently gave herself a Charlie Chaplin moustache. Brice burst out laughing.

'What's funny?'

He picked up a piece of mirror and held it in front of her. Blanche started laughing too, and all the birds which were picking around nearby flew off, saying to themselves that humans weren't people you could mix with, that was for sure.

'Brice, promise me you won't die.'

'I'll do my best, but …'

'Don't believe what they tell you. There's nothing above us, and nothing beneath. Just us, here and now, like survivors of a shipwreck.'

It was ten o'clock when Élie's van dropped them off outside the Montéléger house.

'Goodnight, Brice.'

As she kissed him goodbye, Blanche whispered in his ear, 'That was such a lovely day, wasn't it?' Then she was gone, swallowed up by the shadowy mouth of the porch.

He went to bed as soon as he got home. The cat grumbled and moved a few centimetres when he rolled himself up in his sleeping bag like a large caterpillar in its cocoon and fell into a deep sleep. For a few hours, men, things and animals would be at peace.

He had not washed or changed his clothes for three days. The fact that he smelled didn't bother him. On several occasions someone had rung the doorbell, but he had not answered. Blanche, probably, come to watch 'things' on TV. He was slightly cross with himself, but he couldn't help it, he wasn't able to speak to anyone. After the release of the pheasants he had been seized by a kind of torpor. He slept as much as the cat, waking only to open a tin of food which he shared with it, before plunging once more into a deep coma. His sleeping bag was covered with cracker crumbs, and tins were piling up at the foot of the camp bed. He had run out of clean clothes, and his hair and beard were itchy. When he ran his hand through them, flakes of dandruff fell on to his knees like the scales of a snake sloughing off its skin. He had no tobacco left and nothing edible in the fridge. The situation was approaching a question of life or death, which can be a hard one to answer.

It took him a great effort of will to reach the bathroom. The scalding water hit his body like a jet cleaner hosing a crusty wall. It was like a suicide in reverse; he was coming back to life without really knowing why. It was not unpleasant, if a little violent. The eau de toilette smelled of spring. In a box which was starting to develop mould, he found things to wear. The ecru linen suit, cotton shirt and soft slip-on shoes were inappropriate for the time of year perhaps, but they had the merit of being clean.

The ringing of the telephone made the walls vibrate. It took him a certain time to locate the machine, which he had forgotten existed.

'Hello?'

Amid a chorus of crackling, he thought he could make out a woman's voice.

'It's very difficult to hear you …'

The voice, almost inaudible and stammering out incoherent syllables, '… rice … come … early … ed … ery,' seemed familiar nonetheless.

'Who is this? Hello? Hello? Emma!'

Emma. It was Emma! She was calling from a distance and the line was bad, but it was her, of course it was!

'Emma! Darling, where are you? Emma!'

Then … click. The dialling tone. No more. Bells began pealing wildly in his empty skull. Without understanding what he was doing, he began running around the house from cellar to attic like a lab rat. Really, it wasn't as big as all that, the house – it even had some pieces missing like an unfinished jigsaw puzzle.

At last, out of breath, he caught the cat which was following him in his mad chase and threw it up in the air. 'I knew it! I knew it! Emma's immortal. She'll come back, this evening, tomorrow or the day after, but she'll come back. She has to!'

At the wheel of his little car he carried on laughing fit to burst. He was off to fill the fridge with salmon, caviar, champagne, foie gras, all the finest things, to celebrate her return in due style. At a red light he could contain himself no longer and gestured to a lady driving a Ford to wind down her window.

'Yes?'

'Emma's not dead, have you heard?'

'I'm sorry?'

'My wife, Emma. She's alive!'

'Ah. That's good. Have a good day, Monsieur.'

The lights turned green and the lady roared off.

He had broken down not far from his house, three kilometres perhaps, a distance he covered in driving rain with a bag of provisions in each hand. The fine cream linen suit was reduced to a sopping rag when he reached home, and as for the supple slip-ons, now clarted with mud, they might have been mistaken for common clogs. But what did it matter, since Emma would be back any time now?

When he had put the foodstuffs in the fridge, he got back into his grubby but dry clothes. Recognising his protector's usual scent, the cat came and snuggled up to him, clawing at the holey sweater and purring. The radio had little to impart, only that a hunter had shot the last she-bear in the Pyrenees 'in legitimate self-defence', and in a nursery school three five-year-old kids had battered a little girl of three to death after a sorry incident on the slide. The parents were asking themselves questions. Life, in other words. Brice felt feverish, his head heavy with a doubt which had newly occurred to him. What if he'd dreamed that phone call? It wouldn't have been the first time he'd imagined something. Blurry-eyed, he looked at the table set for two, with candles which cast dancing shadows on the wall. To calm his nerves he had downed four vodkas. He went out like a light with his forehead resting on the tablecloth. He had bizarre dreams in which embryos kicked and punched one another, and meteorites bombarded the Great Bear in a great disturbance of the stars.

He was woken with a start by the two notes of the doorbell. His teeth were chattering, a bumblebee in his head was trying desperately to get out, and his muscles were stretched taut like cords. Waves of shivers ran through him from head to toe. Nonetheless, powered by some unknown energy, he went to open the door, draped in a tartan rug like an old Indian man. Beneath her umbrella, Blanche seemed to have been parachuted out of the depths of the night on to his doorstep.

'Good evening. I hope I'm not disturbing you?'

'Er, no.'

'I was worried. I've come round several times. You don't look well.'

'My car broke down. The rain. I must have caught a cold. Please, do come in.'

Blanche was astonished to see the table set for two, the candles melted halfway down.

'Are you expecting someone?'

'Er ... yes. That's to say, no ... Well, one's always expecting someone. What can I get you? Tea? No, it's too late. Champagne then!'

His every action was clumsy; the rising fever made him tremble. The room had no right angles in it any more. His nose was running. He popped the cork.

'What shall we drink to?'

'I don't know. To those who are here.'

'To us, then?'

'That's right, to us.'

They clinked glasses. Blanche was looking at him out of the corner of her eye, a weak smile on her lips.

'How did you know I would come?'

'I don't know. Intuition, I should think.'

'No, you were expecting someone else. Someone who won't come.'

'Not at all!'

'Your wife?'

'No ... It's just that I had a phone call and ... Oh God, I don't know. I think I'm going mad.'

Fever and alcohol pearled his brow with sweat. He knocked over his glass – his hands no longer belonged to him. From the other side of the table, Blanche was looking at him, without a word. Her outlines had gone, she was dissolving into the cigarette smoke. He could see nothing now, or only distorted objects, things, stuff he would have been hard put to it to name. It was like the time before the end of the world, when everything was still just plans, drafts, rough sketches. Brice took off his glasses and rubbed the lenses vigorously, but it made no improvement.

'Emma went off on an assignment more than two months ago. She was in the hotel in Egypt where they had that awful terrorist attack. They found her papers, and her things, but not her body. Everyone's convinced she's dead.'

'Except you.'

'Yes … Well, to begin with … but for some time now I've had doubts. So that phone call this morning … I don't know what to think any more. I'm beginning to wonder whether I wasn't dreaming.'

'What did she say?'

'It was a bad line. The call only lasted a few seconds …'

'And you're sure it was her?'

'I don't know. I'd have liked it …'

Blanche stood up. Her face showed no compassion for him. She seemed as cold and smooth as a knife blade.

'You should go to bed. I'll ask Élie to come and pick you up in the morning so you can see about your car.'

He woke up howling, his body crushed by the powerful coils of an anaconda. The cat leaped off his stomach, whiskers bristling like foils, while Brice struggled to free himself of the straitjacket his sleeping bag had become. The blue-tinged glow of a new day was seeping in beneath the garage door. It was going to take courage for him to face it. He had a stinking cold, of the sort that leaves you woozy for weeks on end. Shortly before ten, Élie rang the doorbell.

The day was mild and soft. A cotton-wool sky was dabbing at the countryside. Scattered puddles reflected its emptiness. Élie's reptilian head emerged from under the bonnet of Brice's car as he wiped his hands on a filthy rag.

'I thought it was the distributor with all this damp, but it must be something else. We'll tow it to Loquet's.

He's a good car mechanic, a pal, he won't screw it up.'

'It's kind of you to go to so much trouble.'

'It's not me, it's Blanche. Help me fix the tow bar then.'

The seat of Élie's van was as comfortable as a fakir's bed of nails. Rusty springs poked out, drooling yellow foam. Several times Brice caught Élie looking at him from under the peak of his cap, and shaking his head.

'It's extraordinary!'

'What is?'

'How much you look like Louis, Blanche's father.'

'Yes, so it seems. I've been told that before. Did you know him well?'

'We were born a week apart. We went through everything together, school, First Communion, the army ...'

'What was he like?'

'Like you and me. A man.'

'What about Blanche's mother?'

'Sophia? Nothing to tell. She was a foreigner. They come and they go, foreigners. She went when the little one was five or six.'

'You mean she died?'

'That's not what I said. She went, cleared off.'

The van bounced with every bump on the road, as if it had hiccups. The river was veiled in mist.

'What did he do for a living?'

'Nothing, latterly. He squandered what was left of the inheritance. They still had means at that time.

Before that he wanted to be a painter. He had talent. As a small boy he used to paint things so lifelike you'd have thought they were photos – flowers, cherries, animals. Really good. We were from different worlds, but kids don't worry about that. I taught him how to set snares and he did drawings of what I caught, still lifes, he called them. We got on well. He was a good-looking chap. On saints' days all the girls would be flocking round, but he wasn't the sort to take advantage. Painting, nothing but painting … And then we went off to the army, Algeria. He never came back. At least, he wasn't the same.'

Élie swerved to avoid a dog. The sun was trying half-heartedly to pierce the clouds. An aged sun viewed in the wrong light. Élie chewed his lip as if he regretted saying too much, and yet Brice suspected he wanted to tell him more.

'I need a pee.'

He parked in front of what must have been a quarry, a section of mountain cut like a huge cake. Brice took advantage of the opportunity to relieve himself as well. Legs apart, side by side, they watered the chalky rock. That sort of situation brings men together.

'You don't like me much, do you, Élie?'

'What the hell's it got to do with me? What do you want from Blanche?'

'Nothing. She was the first person I met here. We hit it off. I'm married, you know. My wife …'

'Yes, yes, I know. Cigarette?'

'No thanks. You're very fond of her.'

'I've known her since the day she was born, remember. Life hasn't been easy on her. As I said, when Louis returned from Algeria he wasn't the same man. I should say, he was in the commandos. He must have been through a lot to come back looking like a hunted animal. I've seen that same look in a fox's eyes when it's dragged from a hole, prepared for anything, as ready to die as to kill. He had started drinking. He was always living it up in the big cities. We hardly saw each other. He was still painting, but not the same things, stuff you couldn't recognise, nightmares – not the sort of pictures people hang over their fireplace. They sold though.

'One day he came back from Paris with Sophia, who was Russian or Polish, I was never quite sure. She spoke hardly any French but since she never talked to anybody … Louis was mad about her but I don't think it was mutual. Then Blanche was born and Sophia took off. Louis never got over it. He began going out boozing again. From time to time he'd come home. He used to cry in front of the little girl, and then clear off again. You couldn't say he didn't love her, but … Who knows what goes on in people's heads? He was unhappy. That made me sad for the little one. You could say it was me who brought her up for the first few years. Then one day Louis came back, calmer but worn out. He'd given up painting and was drinking more and more, on his own, drowning his sorrows. One morning he decided to clean his gun. That's it. It was about ten years ago now. The inheritance had practically all gone. Blanche had to part with what little she owned in order to keep the house …'

Élie prised the cigarette end from his lips and rolled it between his fingers before grinding it under his boot. Despite his weather-beaten complexion, Brice could have sworn he was blushing.

'I don't know why I'm telling you all this.'

'Maybe it's because I look like Louis?'

'Maybe. Right, let's go.'

After a brief inspection, the mechanic pronounced that the car would be ready in two days. Élie accompanied Brice home without a word. The wind was driving enormous bales of grey cotton wool across the sky.

'Hello? Hello? Is that you, Emma? Tell me!'

The exchange had been even briefer this time, seconds at most, and there was a horrendous crackling noise, as if someone were pan-frying his heart. Now the only sound coming from the phone in his hand was the echo of the voice he supposed to be Emma's, cut off by the dreadful monotonous beep of the dialling tone. What exactly was the good of this machine? To the best of his knowledge, it was supposed to connect you with anybody, anywhere, at any time. But on today's evidence, was it actually doing its job? At the dawn of humanity, just by sticking a shell to his ear the stupidest of bipeds could at least get a direct line to the sea. What progress had been made?

Three blows of his heel and the telephone gave up the ghost. He spread its remains over the floor with the tip of his shoe. There were more reliable ways of getting in contact with absent friends: gongs, foghorns, howling naked on the roof under a full moon, table-turning.

Trampling his phone had partially relieved the headache which had been gripping him since he woke up. Only partially though, because in his mouth there was still an unpleasant taste of something missing. Emma, of course, but something else as well, a sort of whirlpool which, with the noise of a howling tornado, was consuming the incredible heap of junk amid which he lived, or rather had gone to ground in like a badger in its sett.

'Perhaps I'm dead and I don't know yet.'

Immediately his hand went to his heart. OK, so it wasn't Rio Carnival, just an old-fashioned tango, but it was still beating. What, then? There was definitely a leak in the mass of objects behind which he was trying awkwardly to hide. He could distinctly hear a whistling sound, like a punctured tyre. He picked up the cat snoring at his feet but no, it wasn't coming from there. So …? The bell! The bell was no longer chiming, no longer waving its heavy bronze skirt. Panic-stricken, he ran to the window and ascertained that the hands of the clock were stuck at ten past ten, as in every watch advertisement. His hour seemed to have come, on tiptoe certainly, but it was well and truly here. Strangely, although he had invoked it a good number of times in his life, he now no longer wanted it. It was too soon. People didn't die at ten past ten, it was ridiculous. Besides he hadn't done the housework, or made his will. He had to tidy it all up, that whole muddle of things, stuff, bits and pieces … If he could just have a little time to sort out the mess, then he would be ready to discuss it. Valiantly rolling up his sleeves, he confronted the chaos.

Organise, classify … but how? Initially he thought of arranging the jumble in order of size like in a school photograph, the smallest in front and the taller ones at the back, starting with the coffee spoons and ending with the ironing board. That was one solution. Alphabetical order seemed more logical, however. In the beginning was … the abacus. At least that was one thing he could count on. He placed it in the back left-hand corner of the garage.

The task proved as absurd as it was overwhelming, since he was unable to put names to most of the things he was sweating blood to move. Him upstairs had had six days to come up with this shambles, but He was the boss. Without fear of argument, He could pronounce, 'This is a moped, this is a sandal, this is a chick-pea, and that chap there is my son.' Easy in those circumstances to call a spade a spade. In short, Brice succeeded only in replacing one muddle with another.

The cat began exploring the new layout, wasting no time in claiming its territory. How Brice envied it that marvellous ability to adapt.

'Are you sure it suits me, Blanche?'

'Absolutely! You're as handsome as Papa.'

Noting the pitiful state of Brice's wardrobe, Blanche had decided to wash his clothes, lending him some of her father's things in the meantime: a comfortable black velvet suit and a few woollen shirts. He had a little difficulty recognising himself in the bathroom mirror, but there was nothing unpleasant in this sartorial disorientation – quite the reverse. As a child, Brice had loved dressing up, and had owned a most extensive range of outfits going from Davy Crockett to Ivanhoe by way of policeman, fireman or Bozo the Clown. Those pitiful board game compendia, Meccano sets and electric trains received from distant cousins at Christmas had always left him profoundly downcast. He had never understood the pleasure to be had from hours spent watching a miniature locomotive go through a pasteboard tunnel time and time again. The Meccano set with its misleading picture on the lid, suggesting you could build a near life-size model of London Bridge, contained barely enough pieces for a miserable three-wheeled cart. (He had calculated that he would need twenty boxes for London Bridge. At the rate of one Christmas a year, he'd have been about twenty-five by the time he finished his opus.) As for the sets of 1,000 Milestones, Yellow Dwarf, the little horse game and Monopoly, where, like in grammar lessons, you had to follow the rules to the letter or be severely penalised, they necessitated the distressing presence of 'little friends of his own age', usually offspring of his parents' friends, whose very existence he refused to acknowledge. His heroes were all loners: Tarzan (summer only), Zorro, Buffalo Bill, Black Eagle and even the Three Musketeers, since the four of them still made only one.

Who had claimed it was better to die in one's own skin than to live in someone else's? Some megalomaniac philosopher, no doubt.

'You approve, then.'

She was looking at him with tears in her eyes, open-mouthed.

'Is something wrong, Blanche?'

'No … It's just … It's like before, as if he had come back.'

'Well, I'm not a ghost. It's me, Brice.'

'Of course, yes. Can I watch TV?'

'Certainly. Would you like a little Viandox?'

'I'd love some.'

He virtually lived on Viandox, plain in the daytime, and with a little celery salt, Gruyère and soup pasta in the evening. Blanche shared his passion for the bitter bouillon.

While waiting for the kettle to whistle, Brice paced around the kitchen, sitting down and standing up again, bending his knees and elbows like an actor getting into his character's skin, and soon the thick velvet of the suit moulded itself to his shape. He felt completely at ease in it; the pockets were becoming used to his hands. Slipping two fingers into the waistcoat's fob pocket, he pulled out a small piece of paper folded into quarters. A furious scrawl covered a page torn out of a spiral-bound notebook in faded ink: 'Blanche, my child, my dearest, don't be angry with me. I'm so tired …' After that the lines were illegible, presumably blurred by tears. Brice did not try to make out the contents of the note, which had apparently never reached its addressee, but it was easy for him to guess the gist. It was like finding a letter from a private at Verdun in an attic.

As the doorbell rang, he hurriedly refolded the piece of paper and put it back in its place.

Myriam and Simon, his parents-in-law, were standing outside the door, as unexpected as a pair of garden gnomes in the middle of the desert. Myriam opened her mouth, but no sound came out.

'Myriam, Simon? This is a surprise!'

'Hello, Brice. You've changed so much – we almost thought we'd got the wrong house.'

'I expect it's the beard. But come on in, don't stand in the cold.'

They made their way in without a word, eyes fixed on the ceiling like overawed tourists visiting the Vatican.

'I was just making some Viandox, but perhaps you'd prefer tea?'

'Please.'

'Do sit down.'

'Well, it's been quite a while!'

'Sorry?'

'I was saying, we hadn't seen one another for ages.'

'Yes, it's been a long time.'

Myriam was making more conversation than her spouse who, as an expert DIYer, was still assessing the condition of the beams and the quality of the plaster.

'Forgive us for turning up like this, on the off-chance. We're on our way back from visiting friends in Marseilles. We did try phoning you several times but your line must be faulty. It crackles.'

'It's the storms.'

'Ah. You look well enough. The beard and hair, and then those clothes … I won't say they don't suit you, but you do look different.'

It was odd. Everyone here was so eager to recognise him and these people, virtually family, could no longer place him.

'It's the fashion in the country. You look in fine fettle, the pair of you.'

'Touch wood. You can't turn old into new.'

As if to underline the truth of the adage, Simon looked meaningfully at the gaping hole linking the kitchen with the dining room.

'So this is where ...'

'Yes, this is where.'

'It's big! Don't you agree, Simon, it's big?'

'Very! There's still work to be done, but it's got potential.'

'Would you like to see round?'

'Love to.'

As they wandered from room to room, each one emptier and colder than the one before, his parents-in-law shot each other furtive glances increasingly filled with question marks. When they arrived in the attic, which even the spiders had abandoned, Myriam suddenly turned to Brice, her eyes wide.

'But, Brice, where do you live? Where's your room, your studio?'

'I moved into the garage while I'm waiting.'

'Waiting for what?'

'For Emma to come back, of course!'

Myriam opened and shut her mouth several times without managing to produce the slightest sound. Her glasses misted over, her lips began quivering, and she huddled against her husband's shoulder, stifling a sob.

'Come now ... You mustn't say things like that, Brice.

You're hurting everybody, first and foremost yourself.'

'Things like what?'

'You know very well that Emma won't ever come back.'

'Why's that, then?'

'Because she's …'

'Dead? Well, she isn't. She phoned me only yesterday.'

'What are you talking about?'

'Emma's called me, twice.'

'You're insane!'

Myriam broke free of her husband's arms, her face ravaged by sorrow and hatred.

'Crazy! Completely crazy! Emma should never have married you. If you'd been able to make her happy, she wouldn't have gone on travelling the world. If only she'd married someone her own age, she'd have had children, and led a normal life, like everyone else!'

'Myriam, please, let's go.'

'You're a bastard, Brice. A pervert.'

'Come on, Myriam. We're leaving.'

'PERVERT!'

The elderly pair stumbled on the badly lit staircase, hanging on to each other because from now on their life was just a slope without a handrail. Brice felt no anger towards them. He followed them, saddened, shamefaced. Nothing is more moving than the sight of an old couple from the back. Why had he mentioned the phone calls? He no longer believed in them himself. To get rid of Myriam and Simon, no doubt. He was

130

fond of them but they were no longer part of his life; they were dragging him under like a diving bell. In the kitchen, Blanche was boiling water. It was as if a white rabbit had popped out of a magician's hat.

'Hello, Madame, Monsieur. I'm making Viandox. Would you like some?'

Myriam looked daggers at her.

'You see this bastard, Simon? It hasn't taken him long to get another woman in his bed.'

'Myriam …'

The door slamming made the walls shake. He would never see Myriam and Simon again.

'Who was that? Jehovah's Witnesses?'

'No, my wife's parents.'

'They seem nice.'

He leaned against the rock, recovering his breath and massaging his ankle. The sun was honey-glazing the hilltops and bare branches. At his feet the spring babbled the mountain gossip. The water transformed the humblest pebble into a precious stone. Bubbles pearled at the roots of a tree stump shaped like a cow's head. Twigs were borne away by the current. Now and again, down from a bird ripped open by a fox in the night was caught by the breeze, rising and falling like snowflakes on the bushes.

He had slept badly. Garden gnomes armed with pickaxes had assailed him relentlessly. In vain had he destroyed them in their hundreds by hitting them with a phone; more always appeared. Exhausted, he owed his salvation to a tidal wave of Viandox which had drowned them all. With the first glimmer of dawn, he had grasped his stick and set off for the spring, in the hope that nature in her bounty would give him back a little of his taste for life. So far she had only sown treacherous stones on his path, and multiplied the holes and bumps which strained his barely recovered ankle. With a flick of the wrist, his cigarette end drew a near-perfect curve and disappeared into a swirl of green moss.

It was beautiful, and it was sad. It made you want to write a poem, or to shit. He opted for the second. Taking off his trousers he began to push and push, very hard … 'It' was not coming and yet 'it' wanted to come. It would have been the same with the poem, no doubt. The effort made the blood pound at his temples. He closed his eyes and adopted the technique a small dog uses, a series of pants followed by relaxation of the organs. And repeat, several times. It was exhausting but gave him a strange sense of wellbeing. As he crouched there, nose to nose with the tangle of brambles and swarming insects, he became aware of nature's marvellous absurdity. Man had lost his head when he had got up on his hind legs. He had believed that by standing on tiptoe he would distinguish himself from the universal chaos, and had become blinded in his pointless pursuit of conquest. Pathetic little man. All of a sudden he heard a stirring in the thicket. Gently, he moved the branches aside. A few metres away, a fox was wallowing in the remains of an unidentifiable corpse, a thing with fur at any rate, amid a moving cloud of large bluebottles. It would toss it into the air and catch it with its foot or teeth, giving plaintive little yelps. Then, tiring of the game, it threw the stinking remains one last time and left them to the descending swarm of flies. 'That, you poor old thing, is the game you're playing with Emma.' With that, Brice dumped the enormous weight he could carry no longer. It was as if he were giving birth to himself, a stool as large as a lifetime, which was born in a scream and ended in a sigh. He turned round and considered, with some pride, the huge pretzel he had produced.

'There, it's over.'

He could not have said exactly what was over, his grieving perhaps, but it was with a light heart that he made his way back down towards people, the village, teasing the weeds with the end of his walking stick.

Élie was waiting for him outside his door. When he caught sight of Brice he walked towards him. He stopped halfway, shading his eyes with his hand. It was like something out of a Western.

'Hello, Élie. Everything all right?'

'Yes. Your beard, that suit ... It's enough to make me believe in ghosts.'

'It was Blanche's idea. I'd run out of clothes. Were you looking for me?'

'Your car's ready. I can drive you over if you like.'

'That's perfect. I need to do some shopping in town.'

It was true. On his way down from the spring Brice had wondered what would bring him pleasure. Giving presents, it didn't matter what or to whom, as long as he was giving. He was fascinated by Élie's hands on the van's steering wheel. It looked as though he was wearing gloves, old work gloves, cracking and covered in mends. If one day he should kill someone he could always plead not guilty. The hands working the gear lever and scratching his ear or nose were acting on their own, under orders from no one.

'I feel like giving gifts today. What would you like, Élie?'

'A gift? Why?'

'For the car, of course.'

'Oh, that was nothing.'

'I insist.'

'Work gloves, then. Gamm Vert has some on special offer.'

'Right, that's settled.'

'Actually, I was forgetting. Blanche sends word that you're invited to a small celebration at hers this evening.'

'What's the occasion?'

'A small celebration. I'm going too.'

'All right, then.'

Perhaps it was thanks to Élie, but the car repair cost him almost nothing. In town, it was like Christmas. It was a long time since he had mingled with the crowd. It wrapped itself round him like strands of candy-floss. There was a fairground atmosphere. The air smelled of perfume, the lights twinkled, and it was a feast for nose, ears and eyes. And so many colours it was impossible to take them all in. In a shop which sold everything and, more especially, nothing, he bought a miniature television for Blanche. It was scarcely larger than a packet of cigarettes and worked off batteries. At a delicatessen he bought a bottle of champagne and a chestnut gateau.

'Is it for a birthday?'

'I don't know.'

'What shall we write on it?'

'Put … Celebrate.'

'Just "Celebrate"?'

'Yes. I don't know what we're celebrating.'

A little further on, he passed a young mother holding the hand of a little four- or five-year-old girl who was crying and had a hand up to her forehead.

'That's the way it is, Laura. Some doors open by themselves and some don't.'

Learning how the world works can be tough.

At Gamm Vert he found the gloves for Élie on special offer. He took the largest size, almost like baseball gloves. Night had fallen without a sound. One day banishes another. Time was being carried off on the wind. When it begins to blow in the Rhone valley, there's no stopping it. It isn't malicious, rather it intoxicates you, enjoys tripping you up when your arms are full of parcels and, once you've finally succeeded in shutting the door on it, whistles a sly little tune through the keyhole before going off to torment the next person.

'Bloody wind!'

He opened the cake box which had slipped out of his hands. Now the icing-sugar letters spelled only the cryptic message: L … ATE. That no longer had any meaning. He tried to rescue the situation with the tip of a knife but the result was not great, so he gave up. They would be celebrating 'L … ATE.'

The cat came to rub against his legs while he gave his muddy shoes a wipe. Its whiskers were squint, as they were every time it emerged from a very deep sleep.

Brice pulled a tie from a box marked 'Souvenirs' and knotted it under his collar. It was green and wrapped itself round his neck of its own accord. Emma had brought it back from Argentina for him. This was the first time he had worn it. He had never liked it.

'How do I look, then?'

With a yawn, the creature stretched then arched its back and began prowling round its empty bowl.

Blanche opened the door to him. She was wearing a blue apron on which her floury hands had left patterns like cave paintings. Strands of hair had escaped from her clumsy bun and were straggling down her cheeks, which were red and shiny like apples fresh from the oven.

'Quick, come in! What a wind! But ... what's all this?'

'Champagne, gateau – it's in a wretched state, I dropped it – and some little gifts.'

'You didn't need to do that.'

'But aren't we celebrating something?'

'Yes. Leave all that here and go upstairs to get warm.'

Élie was standing in front of the fireplace, hands behind his back. In his solemn black suit, it was as if he were ablaze.

'What a wind this evening!'

'It'll last for three days. Once the dogs are off the leash … How's the car?'

'As good as new. I can't thank you enough.'

'Oh, anyone would have done the same. Did you find the gloves?'

'Naturally.'

'That's good, very good. These hands have had too much use, but I still need them.'

He rubbed them together, oblivious of the flames licking them. They had been cooked time and time again.

'I've brought a pheasant – a proper one, not from the cages. One I bagged myself.'

'Is that what smells so nice?'

'Blanche is a good cook when she wants to be. Her father was very partial to game.'

Blanche joined them. She had just lit the candles in two splendid silver candelabra. Immediately the scantly furnished dining room was transformed into a castle.

'It's beautiful, isn't it? We should dine like this every evening, even when it's herring or noodles.'

Blanche's eyes were shining. With her hands clasped beneath her chin, she looked like an angel straight from a Botticelli painting. A log crackled in the fireplace.

'It's ready. We can take our places. Oh, music!'

She opened an ancient Teppaz portable record player covered in plastic imitation tweed, and slid a record from its sleeve. Very delicately, she moved the arm into position, and, after a few crackles which mingled with those from the log fire, the intro to *Madam Butterfly* echoed round the walls.

'This was my father's favourite piece.'

Élie volunteered to uncork the champagne and they clinked glasses.

'What are we drinking to?'

'It's the anniversary of his death.'

'Oh.'

'To him!'

Blanche was examining Brice with such intensity that he suddenly felt as if he were in bonds, caught in a spider's web. There was something curiously personal about that toast.

The dinner was excellent. The roast pheasant was done to a turn, and its liver spread on crispy toast was sensational. The wines were suitably fine. They spoke of everything or, more accurately, nothing. Élie explained to Brice how to set snares and track a badger or fox. Brice wasn't listening. He could hear words fluttering here and there, and thought to himself, 'Why not be here rather than elsewhere?' It was one more family meal, just like the countless others he had experienced. One life was coming to an end, and he was being given another. Over cheese, Blanche sang a charming lullaby, and when the gateau arrived everyone laughed to see 'L … ATE' decorating the icing.

'Right outside my door, I went to get out my keys and the box flew right out of my hands!'

'I'd love to have seen that!'

Blanche laughed, crumpling her napkin. Yes, a family celebration. That was what anyone who saw them would think. They had known one another for ever, like all castaways, exiles, survivors of the natural disaster life can be. They let themselves be cradled in one of those interludes in existence which make you forget the whys and wherefores for a short time.

Élie coughed into his fist.

'I'm going to have to get going. I'm an early riser. It's been a lovely evening, yes, lovely.'

Brice stood up, not very steady on his feet, slightly tipsy. The embers presented a mesmerising spectacle of Rome burning. Élie extended his huge bear-paw hand.

'Well, goodnight then.'

'Wait! Your gloves!'

It was so dark in the entrance hall that Brice almost gave him Blanche's parcel.

'I took the largest size so you'd be comfortable. They're lined.'

Élie tried them on immediately. Enormous, yellow, they alone were visible as they felt their way in the darkness.

'They're nice, very nice. Thank you.'

Brice needed both hands to shake Élie's one. As soon as the door opened, Élie was gone, whisked away by the wind. Blanche was beginning to clear the table. She was like a moth fluttering round the candles. He held out her gift.

'For you.'

'A gift?'

Blushing, she opened the package but frowned on seeing the miniature TV.

'That … that's very kind, but … does that mean I can't come and watch it at your house?'

'Not at all! You can come whenever you like. That's just, let's say, to help you go to sleep at night.'

She seemed relieved, smiling at him as she clasped the little TV to her chest.

'Then I shall watch it and think of you.'

She planted a butterfly kiss on his lips, closing her eyes. It was very gentle, very cool, vaguely incestuous.

'Right then, I'm off home. Goodnight, Blanche.'

'See you tomorrow?'

'See you tomorrow.'

'Are you leaving?'

    'I'm going into town. Do you need anything?'

    Silence.

    'What is it, Blanche? Is something wrong?'

    'You're leaving …'

She was on the verge of tears. Her lips were trembling and her fingers were clutching the car door so tightly they were turning white. It looked almost as if she was trying to rip it off. Brice got out of his seat and laid his hands on her shoulders.

    'Why are you saying this, Blanche? Look, I've no suitcase inside, no luggage in the boot. Shall I open it for you?'

    'No. But you seem like someone who's running away.'

    'Why would I run away?'

Blanche's eyes resembled two little icy mountain lakes. He didn't know where to put his own. He needed to find a way out of the situation.

'Blanche, I've no reason to hide anything from you. We know each other well now, don't we?'

'I know you,' she said stiffly.

'Listen, I've two or three things to do in town. My phone's not working; I need to buy myself a mobile. You see, there's no need to worry. I'll be back this afternoon. Do you want my keys so you can watch TV at my place?'

'Yes, please.'

'See you soon, then.'

'Yes, see you soon.'

The bell began to ring as he sped off. He didn't count the chimes. It was time, that was all. Without quite knowing why, he had resolved to make a decision. To re-establish contact with his editor, with Mabel and her monstrous child, to resume his previous existence while fully anaesthetised. All he needed was to go home, even if he no longer knew where that was. He would put the house up for sale, at a loss if necessary; he could bear it no longer. He would take a little studio in town, a kennel, a wandering dog's dream. Then there were these strange ties that Blanche was gradually weaving round him. It was as sweet and as dangerous as opium, and so easy to go along with. To be honest, he was totally disorientated, as if each of his legs had decided to go in a different direction. Yes? No? … Yes? No? His state of mind was that of a man playing Russian roulette but with an empty gun.

At Fnac he was shown an endless series of mobile phones, the most modest of which allowed you to view *Star Wars* on a 4 x 2-centimetre screen, photograph your ear and check when your next wee-wee was due.

'Splendid! You haven't anything that allows one to contact another person?'

'Ah, it can also be used as a telephone if you want. It comes in four different colours.'

'Just four?'

Provided you didn't stray off into its multiple functions, the machine did its job very well. He called his editor.

'Hello, Dominique. It's Brice.'

'Brice?'

'Yes. So when do you want your sketches?'

'It's just … as I hadn't heard from you, I gave them to Calot.'

'Calot! The man's useless! Anyway, I *am* Sabine.'

'I know. But what did you expect me to do? I've got deadlines to meet.'

'Give me a date, go on, and I'll send you the lot ready for the printer's.'

'You're a pain, you know. You suddenly come back from the land of the dead and … I'm sorry, I didn't mean to say that. Let's say a week. I'll try and sort things out with Calot. Are you all right otherwise?'

'I'm OK. I'm getting back in the saddle. You wouldn't happen to know of a studio flat to let near you, by any chance?'

'I'll keep an ear out. Are you coming back to us?'

'I'm not sure. I'm thinking about it.'

'I'm glad to see you getting back on your feet. You gave us a fright.'

'Talk to you soon, Dominique.'

His editor's voice seemed unreal. It was a voice from before, one of those he no longer understood, like Myriam's and Simon's, and the supposed messages from Emma. He spent a good hour on a bench in a square throwing pieces of croissant to the ducks. Another house move. Boxes and yet more boxes. Sisyphus's rock hit him in the face once more. He felt he no longer had the courage or the strength or the desire to push it back again. He was leaking like a bucket with a hole in it.

On his return to Saint-Joseph, he had to stop as he approached the Grande Rue. A fire engine was blocking the way. A column of black smoke was rising, sending up swirls of charred particles like a flight of bats. This was the first time he had seen the village's inhabitants all together. They were all outside, young and old, blinking and holding their hands to their mouths.

'What's happening?'

'There's a fire at number seven, the Loriol house.'

Brice plunged into the throng. As he got closer to the incident, smoke gathered in his throat like a Brillo pad. A fireman barred his way.

'Where are you going, Monsieur? You can't stay here, it's dangerous.'

'That's my house ...'

There were no flames visible, only smoke, and the sparks that shot out of the windows from time to time. There was a painful crack and part of the roof collapsed, while a ripple went through the crowd like a Mexican wave. The little men in their chrome helmets battled bravely against the greedy ogre gobbling up the house like a mere chicken carcass. All that could be seen now was blackness. Even the water arcing from the hoses was black.

Blanche collected him from where he stood, wild-eyed, arms hanging limply by his sides, amid the firemen crawling over the wreckage like golden scarab beetles. They reminded him a little of Breton Removals, in a more drastic form.

'You're spending the night at my house. Then tomorrow, we'll see.'

'Yes.'

Blanche's suggestion seemed entirely fitted to the situation. He allowed himself to be led away, like a blind man. The speed with which events were unfolding made any initiative on his part unnecessary. He had only one word left: yes.

'I'll get a room ready for you.'

'Yes.'

'Would you like a bowl of soup?'

'Yes.'

The bowl was identical to the one from which he had drunk his hot chocolate as a child, with a border of blue and white squares, and a chip in almost the same place, as if someone had tried to take a bite out of it.

'Will it be all right?'

'Yes.'

'Have they told you how it happened?'

'A cigarette end or exposed wire, they don't know exactly.'

'Ah. You can stay here for a few days until you've had a chance to think more clearly.'

'That's kind, thank you.'

No, his childhood bowl wasn't blue and white squares, it was yellow and white ... or even red and white.

'The room's ready!'

Spoken like a true soubrette. Blanche absolutely looked the part, spruce, pink-cheeked, sparkly-eyed. Before she resumed an air of sympathy, he could have sworn she was rejoicing in the situation.

It was as if she were on springs. Brice had difficulty keeping up with her on the stairs.

'There, it's this one.'

The room was spacious, with a large bed in dark wood, an impressive wardrobe, a small table, a chair and, on a tray by the bed, an artificial flower in a tooth glass. On the quilt lay a towel and a wash mitt. Blanche pulled back the curtain.

'It's very quiet. It looks on to the cemetery.'

It was a clear night. The rows of little tombs were reminiscent of an outdoor cinema auditorium.

'This is my father's room. No one has slept here since he went. He didn't go far – he's over there, just behind the cypress. Would you like me to run you a bath?'

'No, I just need to sleep. Thank you, Blanche.'

What the hell difference did it make to him whether the room was her father's, the Pope's or Napoleon's? He collapsed on to the bed and removed his shoes by rubbing them against each other, one arm covering his eyes. He couldn't get the taste of ash out of his mouth.

Blackened beams, twisted pieces of metal, shattered windows, melted plastic, objects bloated and reshaped by the fire ... The end of the world had the acrid stench of saucepan bottoms. Through the holes in the roof, the sky glanced in at the debris with the half-curious, half-blasé look of a passer-by. The spectacle was not without a certain charm, rather like a visit to Pompeii on a rainy day. Apart from the insurance – and that would take time since the cause of the disaster was unknown – there was precisely nothing to be salvaged.

What miracle had enabled the cat to escape? It was a mystery. The most likely explanation was that it had found a way out through one of the gaps only it knew about, which make our impregnable fortresses veritable sieves. At all events, Brice had found it marching around in the blackened rubble, looking disgusted and carefully picking up its paws, but without a single hair singed.

'Right, well, that's over.'

Nestled in his arms, the cat gave a grunt of approval to Brice's rigorous summing up of the situation. Goodbye boxes, stuff, whatsits and things: once again he could travel light.

A builder had been called in to make the house safe. The window openings were held in place by timber struts, and metal jacks were propping up the stumps of beams gnawed by the flames.

'We didn't last long together. We can't have been suited. Sorry.'

A tile shattered on the pavement right behind him as he crossed the road.

'And she bears a grudge!'

'It's wonderful, isn't it?'

'What's wonderful?'

'Springtime, and the two of us taking a walk through the vines. It's like before.'

'Before what?'

'Like in Papa's day.'

The sky was like the lid of a sweet jar, the breeze like a baby's breath. The spring *was* pretty, if a little sticky. Everything you touched was dripping with sap – the buds, the grass shoots, even the insects struggling to get out of their chrysalises. Nature was running with amniotic fluid, streaming with glimmering saliva which was polished by the first rays of the sun. Everyone came out of their shells rumpled, amazed, greedy, and drunk on that insolent youth which made them ready to take on death.

Brice was walking in front, lifting flounces of foliage with his stick like a cad lifts girls' skirts. He had been living with Blanche for a month already, and the time had flashed by. There was one place in the house that he was particularly fond of: the attic. It was huge and light. In the past Louis Montéléger had used it as his artist's studio. The bare wooden floor was spattered with multi-coloured splashes of paint. It looked like the aftermath of a carnival. Even in dull weather, the light pouring in through the window was strengthened by reflecting off the whitewashed walls. The only piece of furniture was a sagging old club armchair, its arms torn by generations of tomcats.

The very next day after he moved in, he had put up two trestles and a plank and set to work immediately. In a week he had dashed off the drawings for his editor and received, by return of post, a cheque with the compliments of both Mabel Hirsch and Dominique Porte. He had not derived any pride from it; it left him completely indifferent. He hadn't thrown himself into his work to make money or from virtue, but so as not to think any more, to watch his hand tracing lines and spreading colours from morning till night until his eyes were popping out of his head.

Blanche fussed round him, rather too much. Not an hour went by without her coming to offer him a cup of Viandox, or coffee, or tea …

'No, thank you, Blanche. I'm working. Later.'

'Yes, yes, of course.'

To be honest, after the drawings he hadn't much to do. But he needed to be up there, on his own, with the cat on his knee, sitting in the armchair, gazing at the cemetery. Lonely but loyal old women, their fingers contorted by arthritis, would come to dust and lay flowers on the graves, which were neatly lined up like children's cots. It wasn't sad. It was still life, just. In the distance the crests of the hills stood out like a frieze on the horizon. Absolute silence. It was like being in a glider. Then he would come to himself a little, and for a moment leave behind all the lives he had had. He would dissolve in the pale incandescence of the sky. He lived the life of a cat, with no memory of the previous day and no awareness of the one to come, unable to make any plan at all. On certain days, he might think of Emma, and then he felt a profound guilt, as if by joining the ranks of those accepting the unacceptable, he had killed her with his own hands. In those moments, he would implore her forgiveness with all his heart, but with each passing day her face grew less distinct, becoming blurred as if she wished to be unrecognised in the very depths of his memory. He tried in vain to conjure up a precise recollection of the texture of her skin, her perfume. It was like trying to sculpt smoke, or running water. There *is* a life after death – other people's, of course.

Some might have been astonished by the state in which he was living – vegetative, to put it mildly – but he had no alternative at his disposal. He was quite aware of how precarious his situation was, but what is there that endures if not our incomprehensible, deep-seated need to try to carry on?

Blanche and he would have lunch together. She made him little dishes with the aid of a cookery book. They weren't always a success but then the two of them would laugh about it. After the siesta, which he spent alone, they would go out for a walk, or do some shopping. Blanche had developed a passion for superstores. They would come out with trolleys filled with no matter what. Things in boxes. Back at home they would watch TV, squeezed up in front of the tiny screen of Blanche's television, or read by the fire. They led a family life. Élie came to dinner regularly, once a week, bringing a rabbit, a cabbage, some nuts – the kinds of things people bring to dinner in the countryside. Time, in its monotony, put scars on the wounds.

As they approached the spring, they emerged from the path bordered by thick bushes, dispersing a host of little birds which flew up in a flurry of feathers in search of higher perches. Blanche began leaping from rock to rock with the ease of a mountain goat.

'Come and see, Brice. This is the bath from when I was a little girl.'

He was far from being as sure-footed as she was on the slippery rocks. The memory of his fall was still fresh. He advanced cautiously like elderly people do in winter-time, catching scornful cackles from the bubbling waters every time his foot slipped.

'That's where Papa used to bathe me, you see. Look how smooth the stone is … A bathtub just the right size for me. The waterfall used to come down on my shoulders and make me laugh!'

The pool was shaped like a large font. The water flowing down from the overhang grew calmer for a moment as it eddied, before pouring out through a sort of spout to continue on its way, lower and still lower, level after level, gathering strength and speed as it went.

'We used to bathe stark naked, like savages, Papa and I. We'd play catch, and splash each other. Afterwards we'd have a picnic over there, under the tall pine tree. Once it's warmer the two of us ought to come here for a picnic, don't you think, Brice?'

'That's an excellent idea.'

'One day, Papa …'

'Yes?'

'No, nothing. Let's go home.'

The bathroom was just like a Soviet submarine. As soon as the hot water tap was turned on, the boiler began to splutter and the pipes to shake, loosening a shower of old ivory paint flakes above the washbasin. The showerhead wept a few either icy or scalding tears, because the mixer had not yet invented warm water. Brice was just extracting a blackhead on the side of his nose in front of the mirror when the sound of voices reached him through the air vent. The bathroom was next to Blanche's room.

'You're mad, my poor girl!'

'I'm not your poor girl, Élie! Stop speaking to me as if you were my father! I'm thirty-nine years old, a grown woman!'

'A woman! You're not capable of managing on your own, you know that perfectly well.'

'Exactly. I don't want to be on my own any more.'

'But I'm here, Blanche. Think about it. Brice could be your father.'

'That's what I like about him.'

'You don't know what you're saying!'

'We've got so much in common: things, TV, Viandox. We wouldn't change anything. We'd go on living here.'

'Then what would you gain by marrying him?'

'I'd be able to sleep with him, like with Papa.'

'You should forget all that, Blanche.'

'But I can't! My stomach hurts, and my head, and my heart. And I love him, I really do.'

'What about him? He hasn't finished grieving yet. He doesn't know how to love any more.'

Sobbing ensued, muffled no doubt on Élie's chest. All Brice could see of himself now was a misty man in the steamed-up mirror over the washbasin, with a toothbrush stuck in his mouth.

Brice managed to slip out on the pretext of an appointment with his insurer in town. Blanche had white-rabbit eyes, and Élie ice cubes in the back of his throat, when he left them after coffee.

He lingered in the streets and did a bit of desultory window-shopping, his hands deep in his pockets. He visited the small museum which housed a few of a local artist's daubings, the remains of some Gallo-Roman pottery, a gallery of fossils, shaped flints and arrowheads, and a plethora of stuffed animals in a piteous state in dusty cases: a grey heron, a beaver, a badger, a ferret, a magpie, a rat, the skulls of a bear, horse and rabbit, some frogs, toads and vipers in jars of formalin. The place smelled of wax and dust. He was the only visitor. The floor creaked. Sitting on a cracked leatherette bench, he meditated for a long time in front of the shell of a Polynesian turtle. Polynesia ... islands, trade winds, boredom assured, syphilis guaranteed. Like Gauguin ...

Leaving on tiptoe so as not to wake the attendant asleep on a chair, he made straight for the nearest travel agent's.

'What's the furthest away thing you've got?'

'Furthest away from what?'

'Here, of course!'

'Australia, Tierra del Fuego ...'

'Oh yes, that's good, Tierra del Fuego. How much is that?'

'Well, we have fifteen-day tours.'

'No, just a one-way ticket.'

'I ... Hold on, I'll get you some information.'

He exited the office with a pile as thick as a telephone directory of leaflets and brochures about here, there and everywhere. From there he went to the station and began noting down the times of trains, no matter which, just trains departing. Then he flung the whole lot into a dustbin and went back to Saint-Joseph.

The clock struck seven-thirty as he arrived at the house. Strangely, the lights were off and the kitchen cold.

'Blanche?' he called.

No answer, no one, except the cat which came slithering between his legs, purring. Brice took it in his arms. Just like him, it had grown fatter in the time it had lived here. To be honest, Blanche's absence rather suited him. He had prepared a clumsy speech announcing his departure, while knowing full well he could not avoid the painful ritual of farewell and the plethora of long-winded, pointless explanations. As it turned out, however, fate was holding the door wide open for him. He would have to be blind not to take advantage of the situation. Stealing away like a thief had nothing glorious about it, but it took a certain amount of courage to resolve to be a coward. When a tooth is rotten, you rip it out. He was going to rip himself out.

Packing your suitcase is a relatively simple act, provided you have a case, and something to put in it, which was not true of him. All he owned fitted into an Evian box. He thought of Breton Removals with a pang of guilt. People like him were killing their profession. He made his bed neatly and laid Louis's suit out on top like a recumbent effigy, the jacket sleeves folded on the chest, trousers properly stretched out, legs straight. The cat prowled around, intrigued, as if asking, 'What are you doing?'

'As you see, I'm checking out.'

Then he opened the window so that no smell of him should remain, no sign that he had ever been there. The cat took the opportunity to slip out and disappear over the rooftops without a meow of farewell, without a backward glance. Brice shrugged. That was the way to do it. The moon, half nibbled away by a silver-toothed cloud, was pouring a blue wash over the marble tombstones. All the cypress trees were bending in the same direction, beyond the wall towards the place where there was nothing to see, where darkness swallowed the void, the place he was headed. He wasn't the first to go away without leaving an address. All these tombs were nothing but empty post office boxes.

The Evian box in his arms weighed nothing. He turned the light off. For a split second he saw the room like a photographic negative. He didn't turn on the corridor light, naively believing you vanished quicker in the dark.

Before he had gone three steps into the courtyard, a voice up above him began singing:

'Il était un petit navire
Il était un petit navire
Qui n'avait ja-ja-jamais navigué
Qui n'avait ja-ja …'

Blanche was tightrope-walking along the ridge of the roof, her arms outstretched like a balancing pole, leaning slightly as if she were resting on the wind. A few metres behind her, the cat was peering around the corner of the chimney, its eyes glued to her.

'Blanche! What are you doing up there? Come down at once!'

'No, I'm going away too.'

'But, Blanche, I'm not leaving. This box is … it's things to throw out. Look, I'm putting it down on the ground. Come down. Please?'

Blanche wobbled, like a candle flame in a draught. The cat stretched, and for a moment Brice had a vision of some sort of crazy shadow play, a cruel tale silhouetted against the night.

'Blanche, I wasn't leaving. You've got it wrong. It's windy. You might fall …'

'No. This time it's my turn.'

Blanche crouched down, her elbows resting on her knees and her hands clapped over her ears.

'You're so small … like a tiny ant. You're so far away …'

'No, I'm here. I'm coming up for you. Don't move.'

'One night Maman wanted to go away as well, like you. But Papa didn't let her – he took his gun …'

Blanche aimed her index finger at the moon.

'Boom! Maman stayed. I know where she is. Do you want to know?'

'I don't understand a word of all that. What I want is for you to come off the roof. After that, you can tell me whatever you like.'

Blanche was no longer listening. Again she shot down the moon.

'Boom! I was there. Maman was all floppy when Papa and Élie carried her into the cellar. There were red teardrops all over the steps. Afterwards Papa took me in his arms. He told me no one would leave the house ever again, that I was the queen of the house now, his little Queen Blanche. And then he went away as well. You all leave. Now it's my turn to go.'

With its nose to the roof tiles, the cat was creeping towards Blanche, who was swaying perilously backwards and forwards, singing again: '*Qui n'avait ja-ja …*'

Head tilted back, open-mouthed, Brice had no words left. At that moment, her garbled confessions were a matter of complete indifference to him. It was he who felt dizzy, as if the courtyard paving stones had begun to shake, rising and falling beneath his feet. Just then a car rattled to a halt in front of the gate. Élie appeared, big yellow gloves hanging at the end of his thin arms, a sad Mickey Mouse. Brice was about to take a step towards him when his eardrums were ripped by a terrible growling. He turned round just in time to see the cat leap towards Blanche, who gave a start and lost her balance, rolling down the roof to bounce off the guttering before plummeting ten metres and landing almost at his feet.

There was no longer any oxygen on the planet. Brice was unable to take his eyes off the white patch which was gradually becoming saturated with blood more pink than red. He stood motionless, all his senses frozen, incapable of the slightest thought.

'Clear off.'

At his side, Élie was also staring at the broken doll's body, his expression shaded by his cap. Only his hands shook, as if he had just put down a heavy weight.

'Clear off,' he repeated, 'or I'll kill you.'

Brice did not start breathing again until the Saint-Joseph sign had disappeared in the rear-view mirror. Along the main road the flaking plane trees bowed low as he passed. While stopped at a red light under the bridge across the Rhone, he saw a man making his way out of a cardboard box with the words 'Up' and 'Down' printed on it in red letters. That pretty much summed up the real meaning of life. The man stretched, and scratched his beard. He appeared happy. The light changed to green. Ignoring the hooting from behind, Brice parked hurriedly and ran over to the latter-day cave dweller.

'How much?'

'How much what?'

'How much for your box?'

'Are you a lunatic or something?'

'A hundred? Two? Look, there's three hundred. Scram!'

'What about my sleeping bag?'

'I said move it!'

Flinging the man's few rags after him, Brice moved into his new shell. It stank, but there was a pleasing animal warmth to it.

The Panda Theory

Translated by Svein Clouston

Gabriel is a stranger in a small Breton town. Nobody knows where he came from or why he's here. Yet his small acts of kindness, and exceptional cooking, quickly earn him acceptance from the locals.

His new friends grow fond of Gabriel, who seems as reserved and benign as the toy panda he wins at the funfair.

But unlike Gabriel, the fluffy toy is not haunted by his past ...

paperback: 9781906040420
eBook: 9781908313232
digital audio: 9781910477083

How's the Pain?

Translated by Emily Boyce

Death is Simon's business. And now the ageing vermin exterminator is preparing to die. But he still has one last job down on the coast and he needs a driver.

Bernard is twenty-one. He can drive and he's never seen the sea. He can't pass up the chance to chauffeur for Simon, whatever his mother may say.

As the unlikely pair set off on their journey, Bernard soon finds that Simon's definition of vermin is broader than he'd expected ...

Veering from the hilarious to the horrific, this offbeat story from master stylist Pascal Garnier is at heart an affecting study of human frailty.

paperback: 9781908313034
eBook: 9781908313300
digital audio: 9781910477090

The A26

Translated by Melanie Florence

Traumatised by events in 1945, Yolande hasn't left her home since.

And life has not been kinder to Bernard, her brother, who is now in the final months of a terminal illness.

Realizing that he has so little time left, Bernard's gloom suddenly lifts. With no longer anything to lose, he becomes reckless – and murderous …

paperback: 9781908313164
eBook: 9781908313539
digital audio: 9781910477106

Moon in a Dead Eye

Translated by Emily Boyce

Given the choice, Martial would not have moved to Les Conviviales. But Odette loved the idea of a brand-new retirement village in the south of France. So that was that.

At first it feels like a terrible mistake: they're the only residents and it's raining non-stop. Then three neighbours arrive, the sun comes out, and life becomes far more interesting and agreeable.

Until, that is, some gypsies set up camp just outside their gated community …

paperback: 9781908313492
eBook: 9781908313621
digital audio: 9781910477113

The Front Seat Passenger

Translated by Jane Aitken

Fabien and Sylvie had both known their marriage was no longer working. And yet when Sylvie is involved in a fatal car accident, her husband is stunned to discover that she had a lover who died alongside her.

With thoughts of revenge on his mind, Fabien decides to find out about the lover's widow, Martine, first by stalking her, then by breaking into her home. He really needs to get Martine on her own. But she never goes anywhere without her formidable best friend, Madeleine ...

paperback: 9781908313638
eBook: 9781908313744
digital audio: 9781908313812

The Islanders

Translated by Emily Boyce

It's a few days before Christmas in Versailles. Olivier has come to bury his mother, but the impending holidays and icy conditions have delayed the funeral.

While trapped in limbo at his mother's flat, a chance encounter brings Olivier back in touch with childhood friend Jeanne and her blind brother, Rodolphe.

Rodolphe suggests they have dinner together, along with a homeless man he's taken in. As the wine flows, dark secrets are spilled, and there's more than just hangovers to deal with the next morning ...

paperback: 9781908313720
eBook: 9781908313881
digital audio: 9781910477120